"If you ever need to talk, let me know. And my colleague works with biofeedback therapy—it's been shown to help with PTSD."

"I'll look into it." Tension leached from his muscles. Something about having Garnet plastered to his front. He could get used to holding this woman. And focusing on that rather than how all over the place his reactions were today... Yeah, Garnet won out, for sure. "Should have had lunch at the base lodge lounge."

"Probably."

Caleb tilted her chin up with his finger. "That way we'd have a good chance of standing under that stupid mistletoe."

"Oh." She gasped. "I thought you meant..."

"I didn't."

"You meant—" Her lids lowered to half-mast and her lips parted.

"I meant I'd love the pretense so I could kiss you right now."

* * *

SUTTER CREEK, MONTANA:
Passion and happily-ever-afters in Big Sky Country

Dear Reader,

I love how the holiday season lends itself perfectly to the romance genre—the journey of two characters falling in love is made that much richer by sharing traditions with family, both the ones we're born into and the ones we make ourselves. December in Sutter Creek is festive overload, with snow and community activities and long nights that lend themselves to cozying up by the fire.

Avalanche survivor Caleb Matsuda is new to town, and volunteering to organize the workplace holiday party will fast-track him to discovering his place in the small community. But his co-planner, holistic practitioner Garnet James, is more than a trove of local know-how—she's outdoorsy and adventurous and everything he was attracted to prior to getting buried in a snowfield. Exactly what he needs to heal, provided he can learn to risk again.

Garnet has fears of her own; she intends to slough her chameleon habits and avoid love. Impossible to do in the presence of mistletoe, candlelight and holiday magic. I hope getting to spend Hanukkah and Christmas with Caleb and Garnet brings you joy. Please come find me on Facebook and Instagram—I'd love to hear from you!

Happy reading,

Laurel

Holiday by Candlelight

Laurel Greer

HARLEQUIN® SPECIAL EDITION

Recycling programs
for this product may
not exist in your area.

ISBN-13: 978-1-335-57423-7

Holiday by Candlelight

Printed in U.S.A.

Raised in a small town on Vancouver Island, **Laurel Greer** grew up skiing and boating by day and reading romances under the covers by flashlight at night. Ever committed to the proper placement of the Canadian *eh*, she loves to write books with snapping sexual tension and second chances. She lives outside Vancouver with her law-talking husband and two daughters. At least half her diet is made up of tea. Find her at www.laurelgreer.com.

Books by Laurel Greer

Harlequin Special Edition

Sutter Creek, Montana

From Exes to Expecting
A Father for Her Child
Holiday by Candlelight

For Shellee, Deana and Erin.

Hugs + wine + GIFs = word fuel

Thank you for keeping my tank full
and for being the first to tell me to keep writing.

Chapter One

Caleb Matsuda wiped his boots on the mat inside the door of the coffee shop and held back a self-directed scowl. One of these days, he'd walk in here and feel like a local instead of a tourist. He'd better, given how much he'd sunk into his new partnership at the Sutter Creek Medical Clinic—how much he counted on this town helping him heal.

Today's meeting will be another step toward fitting in.

Healing, well, that'd take a bit more than planning a holiday party.

Fixing a smile on his face, he brushed snow off his wool coat and wiped melted flakes from the lenses of his glasses with his gloved thumb. He scanned the cozy tables for Garnet James's habitual cloud of curly auburn hair, but the only flashes of red came from the shop's holly-and-tinsel Christmas garland.

Maybe she had a punctuality problem to go along with her free-spirited reputation. He'd met her a few times since moving to Montana, not many. Adjusting to being a family physician instead of a surgeon took most of his emotional energy. He hadn't made enough strides to build his social network yet. Garnet had always been congenial, though. She was in tight with his two closest friends in town—fine, his *only* two friends—who swore she was the friendliest person on the ski patrol.

Hopefully that was the truth, considering Caleb had

volunteered to work side by side with her for the next couple of weeks. The medical clinic and the holistic health center where Garnet worked part-time were planning a joint holiday party, a celebration of the ongoing close relationship between the two facilities' staffs. But according to Garnet's panicked email, some sort of glitch meant they suddenly didn't have a venue. She and Caleb had been tasked with finding a replacement. Surely her concern was misplaced. Couldn't be that hard to find a replacement in a sleepy mountain town.

Jamming his gloves and knit cap in his pocket, he made his way over to the short lineup and perused his options from the chalkboard behind the elf-hatted barista.

An elbow nudged him. "Still enough of a newbie that you need to read the menu?"

He straightened and turned toward the source of the lightly teasing voice. Yep, just as he'd remembered. Gray eyes like a summer storm. Vibrant hair tucked under an oversized, hand-knit hat. A wide smile and a handful of freckles took her from model pretty to interesting. A couple years ago, he'd have dived in headfirst—the outdoor-healthy vibe she had going on used to be exactly what he looked for in a woman. A guy could get addicted to her wide, generous smile.

She was damned easy to look at.

But her ski-addict lifestyle was hard for Caleb to even think about.

"Me and the flatlanders," he volleyed back, feeling his smile stiffen at the words. Hopefully no one could see he was carrying around enough baggage to stop a 747 from getting airborne.

Her brows drew together under her turquoise beanie. "I thought you were from Colorado."

A lump clogged his throat. Denver just represented loss to him now.

She cocked her head and a loose curl fell across her cheek. "You okay?"

Coughing to get rid of the memories blocking his airway, he said, "I'm from Brooklyn, originally."

"Yeah, I can see New York on you." Her eyes danced as she gave him an exaggerated once-over. "Fancy duds, Matsuda."

His cheeks heated and he shrugged. Maybe he needed to temper his need to look nice with Sorel boots and layers of Gore-Tex in an attempt to blend in with the locals. "It's my lunch break. I dress up for work."

A hint of heat flickered in her eyes. Did she appreciate the effort? It'd been a while since a woman had looked at him with interest, or at least since he'd noticed it—

And there was no point in figuring out the meaning of the sparkle in her gaze. Nothing about Garnet James was good for him. They had zilch in common. Despite his choice to keep living in the mountains—a failed attempt at exposure therapy after the accident—he had no plans to set foot on the slopes again in this lifetime.

She clapped her hands, her mittens muting the noise. "Speaking of work, we have our fair share to do. We should order. I worked here part-time until I started at the wellness center in September. I can vouch for the eggnog latte and the cheese scones. And the vegetarian croissant is amazing."

Once they had coffees and sandwiches in hand—well, sort of in his case, since the lack of mobility in his right hand meant he had to awkwardly prop his plate between his palm and his stomach—he motioned her ahead. Most of the tables were lunch-rush full, but she had a couple to pick from. "Lead the way. Do you have a regular spot?"

Gray irises sparkled silver. "I live to be spontaneous."

His earlier nervous stomach returned. Spontaneity wasn't for him anymore. Being an adrenaline junkie had cost him his surgical career.

Damned useless.

He stopped the thought. Not useless, just different. Still valuable.

And planning this party would help him make some connections. Feel part of something productive, less of an outsider at work and in the small town he was trying to make his home.

He followed her to a four-seater, put his plate down with as much grace as he could manage, then flexed his hand. Garnet's gaze landed on his stiff, scarred fingers, but her wince held no pity, no hint of condolence. Just a pure empathy that he probably should have expected from someone who worked in both emergency services and holistic healing.

Her smile... Man, it warmed an inner part of him. One that had been mighty chilly since his ex-girlfriend had broken up with him—as soon as enough time had passed following the avalanche that leaving him no longer seemed tacky. Something uncomfortable shifted in his chest. Something he'd label attraction if he didn't know better.

Uh, no way. Shrugging out of his coat, he took a seat.

"I'm so sorry for the venue problem. Everyone at Evolve is," she said, naming the wellness center. She scrunched up her face. "I know it was on us to organize that, but the person who volunteered got a job in Jackson Hole. Left us high and dry for reflexology *and* party planning. And when I realized she hadn't even called around to book a place..." She cupped her drink with both hands and took a sip. "Well, needless to say, we're kind of up a creek."

His mouth twitched. "Time to put on our life jackets?"

"Might not be quite that dire, but close."

"Should we cancel?"

Garnet's face fell. "Oh, we can't… I want to introduce a new tradition. Hopefully amplify the camaraderie between Evolve and your clinic, work together where we can."

His gaze wandered to the fake snow sprayed along the edges of the leaded window panes that ran the length of the wall. Similar to the presents and snowmen painted on the windows of the clinic, and the glittery swag hanging behind the receptionist's desk… "Yeah, you're right. My coworkers will be pissed if they don't get a Christmas party."

The last thing he wanted was to be the new guy *and* the person who cheated them out of their holiday festivities.

"Do you want it to be more of a generic winter theme?" she asked cautiously. "Zach mentioned you were Jewish."

He lifted a shoulder. "When in Rome. Or small-town Montana, rather. I figured volunteering for this would help me get to know Sutter Creek better. And if we plan a potluck, I bring *sufganiyot*. Jelly donuts."

She shook her head. "I would lie down in the street for donuts, especially homemade, but we are *not* going the DIY route."

"I didn't realize it would be so involved. I figured we'd book out the pool table section of the hotel lounge and be done with it," he said.

Her mouth tugged to the side for a second, then relaxed, as if she'd gone to bite her lip and then ordered herself not to. "I can take the lead and delegate specific things. *Classy* things," she repeated.

"Fill me in, then."

"I have a list. Aside from a venue, we need to arrange catering, decorations, entertainment…"

All things for which he had no frame of reference in his new hometown. Google was clearly going to become his friend.

"First, we need to hammer down a location," she said. "And the only place I could find that has space in two weeks is the Peak Lounge up the mountain."

He swore the instrumental version of "Silent Night" playing over the speakers overhead made a needle-on-a-record screeching stop.

Up the mountain? The back of his neck prickled, and he breathed through his nose to regain his calm. Oh, man. Could he get away with sneaking out for fresh air before the ambient restaurant noise started to sound like the crack and rumble of snow sliding down a hill?

Garnet's lips moved—saying his name, maybe? After a few seconds, soft music filtered back into his buzzing ears. He rubbed a hand down his face, hoping to get blood flowing back into his cheeks.

"The view is incredible," she said. "And we'll be able to have a dance floor."

"There have to be other options," he murmured.

"Not that I know of."

He couldn't stop his cheek from flinching. "We should at least call around."

"I *did* call. I have a list and everything." Sighing loudly, she took a notebook from her purse. With a shove, she slid it toward him. It knocked into his coffee, tipping the to-go cup onto the pad. Dark liquid poured out the peel-back spout of the lid. Righting the cup, he stood quickly to avoid getting a lap full of scorching coffee.

"Oh, no!" Garnet grabbed a stack of napkins and

dabbed at the spill, smearing the ink on the page. "Did it get on you? I'm so sorry. I'll get you another one."

"Don't worry about it." After sitting back down, he took his own napkin and wiped the table, adding to the sodden napkins she'd piled in the middle of the table. "Probably better if I avoid the caffeine. Might need a new copy of your notes, though."

They both reached for the damp notebook at the same time, hands colliding. Instinctively, he covered hers with his uninjured fingers.

Her gaze snapped to his, wide with surprise. With something else, too, something warm, magnetic.

Heat flooded his veins. Her skin, soft and warm and contrasting with the strong tendons underneath—the mark of a woman who worked with her hands—pulled him in.

He couldn't let go for the life of him.

She didn't seem to have the same problem, slipping her hand from under his. "We don't have time to wait to book. We're lucky anywhere had room on a Friday in December."

He let out a slow breath. He wasn't being purposefully difficult. Hell, two Decembers ago he'd have been the one pushing for a party up a mountain. But if this one was held anywhere in the vicinity of a building with the moniker "Peak," he wouldn't be able to attend. Less than helpful for one of the planners.

"You're sure the lounge at the Sutter Mountain Hotel doesn't have room? I, uh, don't know anywhere else suitable," he said, earning a raised brow. But any topic was preferable to dwelling on his inability to climb on a chairlift. Even admitting that he barely knew where to buy groceries here, let alone where to host a get-together for fifty-odd people. "And you called every restaurant in town? And the smaller hotels? If there's anywhere you missed, I'll phone around after my last appointment."

"I've done that already." Her teeth latched onto the edge of her petal-pink lower lip. "Not going to lie, my heart's set on the Peak Lounge. The ceilings are killer, and the price is right. My bosses have a bit of an in." Her mouth quirked.

"Couldn't those same bosses get us an in at the Loose Moose?" he said, throwing out the name of the local bar also owned by the Dawson family's company. Alpine-Peaks had a laundry list of businesses to its name, from Evolve Wellness and a handful of eating establishments to the entirety of Sutter Mountain Resort. Not to mention, Caleb could credit the Dawsons—well, Lauren, at least—for his position at the clinic.

He'd been drowning in Denver, working as an ER physician in the hospital where, prior to the avalanche, he'd made his name as a trauma surgeon. He'd come home from a twenty-one-hour shift, sick to death of people sending sad, fleeting looks at his injured hand. His call to his buddy, Zach, Sutter Mountain's ski patrol director, had been intended as a stress release. But Zach had mentioned his soon-to-be sister-in-law was bailing as clinic partner and they needed someone to fill the position, stat. Caleb had called the managing partner before changing, showering, napping, anything.

Four months later and the job still seemed like a lifeline. But he wouldn't truly settle in until he could claim resident status. Which he wouldn't earn if his issues hampered his coworkers' traditions.

He ran his fingers through his hair, racking his brain for an impersonal reason not to have the party up the mountain. "People aren't going to want to schlep up two chairlifts in their holiday finery."

"There's a gondola, silly."

Gondola, chairlift... Didn't make a difference for him. "Still a lot of effort."

"But the Moose?" She blinked at him, a slow sweep of long black lashes that fanned out over—

Wait, what? Whoa, Matsuda, stay on topic. "My knowledge of appropriate places is minimal. I know next to nothing about the town..."

Her eyes lit. "Tell you what—we can make a trade. I'll book the Peak Lounge, and in exchange, I'll take you around, show you some of Sutter Creek's highlights. God, in December? You're in full-fledged small town–charm season."

He couldn't do more than scowl to cover up the bolt of fear that zigzagged through his body. Getting a tour around town sounded great, but her proposed cost? Way too high. He shook his head.

"Work with me here," she cajoled.

Damn. Was he going to have to admit how he felt about heights? Sweat dampened his forehead and he tried to subtly wipe it away with the back of his hand. "Garnet, I—I can't."

Chapter Two

"You can't," Garnet echoed. He was just going to leave it at *can't*? Seriously?

But the person fighting not to break into a sweat in front of her was not the calm, serious man she'd met a handful of times while hanging out with her friend Zach. When she'd walked up to Caleb at the counter earlier, he'd seemed his usual self: reserved to the point of approaching stoic, and put together as hell. His charcoal wool coat had cut a perfect line over wide shoulders and a tall, rower's build. Dark hair curling over the arms of his thick-rimmed glasses. With that coat and his impeccable leather boots, he should have looked out of place. Sutter Creek was quaint and quiet, a Western-rustic mix that didn't lend itself to urban swagger. But Caleb carried himself like a man at ease in whatever space he happened to be occupying.

The sheen on his forehead hinted that she'd been wrong on that assessment.

"I—" His paper coffee cup dented as he gripped it and glanced to the side.

She waited for him to elaborate, but he didn't.

Not that she could blame him. He probably wasn't in the habit of admitting personal details to a woman he barely knew. She'd been told once or twice she overshared and shouldn't expect everyone to do the same. She cupped her mug, focusing on the heat seeping into her palms as she echoed, "You can't?"

His lips wobbled for a fraction of a second before he twitched the corners of his mouth up and nodded.

A minuscule movement.

But Lord, it packed a wallop. Something about that clean-shaven jaw begged for a finger to be dragged along his olive skin.

Her mouth felt like she'd stuck her wool mitten inside it. She moistened it with her tongue. Enough of that. Garnet had been operating on a look-but-don't-touch basis on the dating front for the last few years, which had made her life a hell of a lot easier. She had no plans of abandoning the strategy anytime soon. Not if she wanted to stay true to her own goals and desires. "Okay, what *can* you do?"

"The rest of the legwork to find somewhere else to rent." He absentmindedly massaged the fingers of his right hand, which looked hella stiff. His cheek flinched, and tightness pulled at the corners of his dark brown eyes.

The few facts she already knew about him knitted together with what she was seeing. Sympathy spread through Garnet's chest. Apparently, the guy had been a top-notch surgeon in Denver before he moved to Sutter Creek a few months ago. Rumor was he now spent his off time holed up in the massive, too-modern-for-the-surroundings house he'd bought himself out on Moosehorn Lake. How many times had she heard people gossiping about Caleb while picking up a loaf of Nancy's famous sourdough at the bakery? *The new doctor, so handsome—I heard he was in an avalanche. The one that killed Cadie's husband. Someone told me he was a skier but I've never seen him up the mountain.*

Not surprising. In Garnet's patrolling and search and rescue work, she'd seen the impact avalanches could have on survivors, including preventing people from wanting to strap on skis again. PTSD was common. Garnet both understood how traumatic getting caught in a slide could be and at the same time couldn't fathom not spending most of her winter days in the snow. Was that the source of his hesitance? Even though a staff party wouldn't involve any skiing?

Well, crap. She had to have a venue by this afternoon. "I get you're reluctant, but delaying much longer will mean losing the one remaining available place that can handle our numbers. If we want to get our coworkers dancing to 'Livin' on a Prayer' with candy-cane martinis in their hands, we need to make some decisions."

He checked his watch, a brushed silver design with enough dials to look like it belonged on the dashboard of one of the mountain's snowcats.

Irritation flared behind her breastbone. "Somewhere better to be?"

He cocked a dark brow. "I only have thirteen minutes to hoof it through the crowds of Thursday skiers and holiday shoppers. Locals are still making appointments to get a read on the new guy in town. Add in a few tourists who went too hard on the mountain and are regretting it, and my afternoon's packed."

Her stomach twisted. What if he went back to the clinic and complained about the meeting, about her being stubborn or unpleasant…? *Doesn't matter.* Her chest tightened, and she forced herself to take a breath. *You're not responsible for others' opinions of you.* She was beyond changing herself to fit in.

He needed to respect Evolve, and follow through with whatever tasks he took on for the celebration. Beyond that? Irrelevant.

"I need another hour of your time, Caleb. We haven't decided on anything."

"Another day. After I've done some research."

Calm. Breathe. You've got this.

The bakery gossip floated back into her mind. *Never seen him up the mountain...*

Maybe she needed to play along in order to get him to see how much of a pinch they were in. "You know, you're living up to the stubborn surgeon stereotype by needing to do the work yourself to believe it's true, but if you want to waste your time, fill your boots."

His shoulders dropped an inch. "Thanks. I'll let you know what I find. And also..." He held up his right hand, a grim look on his face. "I'm not a surgeon anymore."

Her breath hitched. She could have blamed the shock on the network of red marking his fingertips, palm and wrist. But scars didn't faze her.

His openness, though? And wanting to hold that hand, to trail her hand up his forearm and across the thin, teal sweater covering his hard pecs?

Ding ding ding. We have a winner.

Or rather, loser, if she allowed herself to be attracted to yet another guy with whom she didn't share interests.

"Have you tried acupressure?" One of the reasons she'd been so excited to see Evolve open was to allow people in their small town to access a wide range of alternative therapies that they'd previously had to drive the forty-odd minutes to Bozeman to access.

"Yes." A hollow smile played at the corners of his mouth. "I've tried everything." He shot to his feet and yanked his hat onto his head. His jaw hardened until it looked about as flexible as the crag over by Devil's Playground that she liked to climb during the summer months.

"I had my hand crushed between a tree and a rock. Pretty sure it's normal to have pain."

"Yeah, but—"

"I still have your email address from arranging this meeting. I'll send you a note after I finish calling places. Have a good afternoon." Grabbing his coat off the back of the chair, he strode out of the cafe like an elk was charging him.

Okay, then. Not so open, maybe.

And not so stoic as she'd thought.

She'd give him a day to call around. Maybe even two, just to be generous. She knew the lounge's event coordinator well enough to ask the guy to give her a heads-up if anyone else was interested in the date of the party. And in the meantime, she'd try to get a better read on Caleb Matsuda's mental wellness.

The next day, Garnet headed into the Evolve staff room before her Friday afternoon shift. Spending yesterday evening working on people with varying injuries and health issues had only reinforced the curiosity she felt over Caleb's emotional walls. Seeing him in pain grated on her inner healer. Good grief, doctors were the worst at not taking care of themselves.

Luckily, she had an inside track with the small number of people who knew him beyond acquaintance. Two of whom were sitting at the round lunch table, heads bent over a binder thick with clippings and snippets of ribbons and fabrics. Details for Lauren Dawson's wedding, no doubt. Lauren and her sister, Cadie, had been juggling the management of Evolve and the planning of Lauren's New Year's Eve nuptials for months.

And given Lauren and Cadie had been all over using their familial connection to book a venue, they might be willing to brainstorm ways to work around Caleb's reluctance. But it didn't seem polite to jump straight into "Hey, can you do me a favor?"

"How many days until W-Day?" she asked, gesturing at the bursting-at-the-seams wedding binder.

Lauren straightened, hands resting on top of her rounded belly. Her blond hair was pulled into a bun and she wore leggings and a long T-shirt. "Twenty-nine. I'm not sure what I'm more excited about, though. The baby, or the wedding. Being pregnant at my height, I swear, I looked full-term at four months. And I'm hitting that third trimester energy suck."

"With two months to go? Sleep now, or forever hold your peace," Garnet said, smiling.

Lauren glowered.

"Are you and Tavish signed up for this month's labor-and-delivery support class?" She, along with a few of her copractitioners and a local midwife, was offering a joint session on pain management during childbirth. "Or does it conflict with your wedding chaos?"

"We'll be there." Lauren's face turned cautious. "I have a serious case of knowing too much, I think. I'm paranoid I'll need an epidural and that I'll end up with a C-section, and I want to avoid that." Rolling her shoulder, she winced. "And I have a knot in my shoulder the size of a watermelon."

"That's your *stomach*, Laur, not your shoulder," Cadie said, brown ponytail bobbing in time with her laughter.

Garnet cringed but Lauren just rolled her eyes and flipped her sister off. "One of these days Zach's going to knock you up and you'll be the one suffering. And it'll be your second, so you'll be even bigger."

Cadie stuck out her tongue. "Slow down there, Speedy Gonzalez. We don't all end up engaged in the time it takes us to sneeze. And Ben's not even eighteen months old. I don't see getting pregnant quite yet."

Taking in the classic give-each-other-crap routine, Garnet's heart panged. In the last six months, Lauren had fallen back in love with her high school boyfriend, Tavish, and the couple was thrilled about their less-than-planned pregnancy. And Cadie had found the courage to find love with Zach, her late husband's best friend. The two of them were too cute together, especially when Cadie's son was around. Garnet could not get enough of watching Zach, normally the mountain's cool-as-a-cucumber ski patrol director, turn to mush when he was with Ben.

God, it would be amazing to have such a close family. Garnet usually didn't mind being an only child, but sometimes she ran up against a reminder that there was nothing quite like that bond.

Lauren rolled her stiff joint again, and Garnet sent her a sympathetic look. "Want me to work on that for a few minutes?"

"Ooh, please."

Garnet set to loosening the tight band of muscle. "Maybe not a watermelon, but at least a grapefruit."

"Oh, my God." Lauren moaned with pleasure. "I'm marrying the wrong person."

Garnet laughed.

Cadie focused in on Garnet. "How did your meeting with Dr. Do-Me go yesterday?"

Garnet involuntarily tightened her grip on Lauren and a hiss rent the air.

"Oh, dang, sorry," she apologized.

"That did the trick, I think. I felt it give just then," Lauren said. "But don't stop for that reason, please. And what went wrong during the meeting?"

"He crapped on my idea of holding it up the mountain. I need a way to convince—what did you call him? Dr. Do-Me?"

Cadie grinned. "He did some of the medical support on Sam's films. Rumor has it that was his nickname on set."

Easy to believe. Those troubled eyes alone could coax a woman between the sheets.

"I tried to set you up with him, Cadie," Lauren said.

"I know." Cadie's expression softened to a dreamy musing. "And I ended up right where I was meant to be."

Another throb pulsed in Garnet's chest, followed by a spear of fear to her gut. How did people survive in relationships without losing themselves? She'd certainly never managed to do it.

She withdrew her hands from Lauren's shoulders and took a seat at the round table. "If either of you have any inside information, fill me in."

Mirrored cocked brows betrayed the sisters' blood relationship, and that they'd both read Garnet's intent wrong.

"Not for personal interest. Good grief. I'm still happy not dating." Well, "happy" might be exaggerating. Content, out of necessity. "I want to know how to get him to agree to rent out the Peak Lounge."

Cadie tilted her head. "Why does it matter so much?"

Defensiveness rose, and Garnet tamped it down. It was a logical question, not an unreasonable request for Garnet to justify her decisions. She'd promised to stop doing that.

She wasn't a chameleon anymore. A girl only needed to wake up with her throbbing, hungover head resting on a random dorm toilet once to realize that making choices based on others' interests was stupid at best.

She'd left that behind when she left grad school, and had been learning who she was and what she liked since. Juggling her acupressure practice, her ski patrolling and her work with search and rescue would prove she'd figured it out. Also, staying away from the opposite sex until she could know she wouldn't throw her interests aside for a set of strong shoulders.

"Nowhere else has space, not on the last weekend before Christmas. And I really want Evolve's first holiday party to be great." The image of a sheen breaking out on Caleb's forehead surfaced in her mind. "I don't want to force the issue if it's triggering him, though."

"Triggering?" Lauren asked.

"I'm not an expert, but his behavior reminded me of an ex-soldier I've worked with. And PTSD isn't an uncommon response to an avalanche."

Cadie paled.

"Crap, sorry for bringing it up, Cadie." Her late husband had died in the same Whistler backcountry slide that Caleb had been caught in, and Zach, who'd been onsite but hadn't been swept up, had dealt with some major survivor's guilt.

"No, it's okay." Cadie's throat bobbed. "It's a tricky balance, figuring out how hard to push people to heal. I should know. Zach and I almost didn't get together because we were both stuck in emotional stasis. I hope Caleb's not still there."

Garnet sensed he was, but it didn't feel right to speculate further. She sucked in a breath. "Well, I'll have to be strategic, then. If going up a mountain is a mental health block for him…"

"Given I was ready to give you an engagement ring after you rubbed my shoulder for a few minutes, I'm putting my money on you getting through to him," Lauren said.

"Yeah, but I'm using words with him, not acupressure treatment."

"You'll do right by Evolve, Garnet. I know it. And I'll

save a week's worth of energy to make sure I can dance up a storm." Lauren rose, yawning. She turned to her sister. "I don't think I can handle hitting the lodge lounge after work tonight. I need to go to bed at like, five."

Cadie made a sulking face, then laid a wheedling smile on Garnet. "How about you come? Otherwise it's just going to be me and all the patrol crew."

"I'm part of the patrol crew," Garnet reminded her friend.

"You don't count. You talk about things other than who got first tracks where and blah, blah, blah."

"Oh, as if you don't get all warm around the edges when Zach's in his uniform," Garnet teased. She really shouldn't say things like that—Zach was her boss for her part-time patrol hours, after all. But the appeal of a guy in a red jacket skiing a curling ribbon of turns into fresh powder couldn't be denied.

It was entirely an objective observation.

Unlike the warmth she'd felt around Caleb Matsuda. She'd reacted far beyond objective appreciation. And for the sake of her equilibrium, she could not entertain that.

Cadie crossed her arms. "I may be guilty of having locked Zach's office door once or twice when he was decked out in sexy gear. And I'm demanding payment for that admission—you're coming with me for drinks later. Zach's sister is visiting, and we promised her we'd actually be fun given it's Friday. Dad's watching Ben, and I don't want to waste a babysitter night surrounded by testosterone and tourists."

"That'll probably be the theme of the night, even if I am there," Garnet said.

"So you're going to desert me, too?" Cadie complained.

"I didn't say that. But I'm not going to dilute the hormones and general air of hookups all that much."

Cadie pointed a finger at Garnet. "I'll take it."

And Garnet would take the certainty she wouldn't run into Caleb at the lounge. She'd never seen him hang out with Zach while Zach was with the mountain crew.

She needed time to prepare before she ran into the sexiest man in Sutter Creek again.

Chapter Three

Caleb slammed down the handset on his office phone. Spending his Friday lunch hour working through Garnet's coffee-stained list had proved he didn't know a thing about the restaurant industry. As all the hosts he'd spoken to had informed him, their managers and event coordinators weren't available during dinner service. But he needn't bother calling back—every place was booked to the last table on the weekends in the lead-up to Christmas.

Scratch that—the Loose Moose was available. But Garnet had protested hard when he'd thrown it out as an option. He put his chances of convincing her to hold the party at a scuzzy bar between zero and nil.

Unless they were going to get really creative, she'd be getting her way. And he'd be getting left out.

He leaned back in his chair. A wave of homesickness swamped him. Not a longing for Denver, for the sterile condo and sixteen-hour—if he was lucky—days at the hospital.

He missed his parents' brownstone. And the trip back to New York he had planned for the end of January seemed a hell of a long way off.

Rubbing his breastbone, he pulled out his cell and dialed his mom's number. Three fifteen East Coast time on a Friday? She'd be in the kitchen, no doubt, directing his brothers in preparing the culinary masterpiece she spent every Friday afternoon making. No matter how busy her medical practice got, family came first, and you didn't get more "family" than sharing Sarah Klein-Matsuda's Shabbat dinner.

"Mom, hey."

"Caleb!" He heard the hiss and clunk of a tap being shut off. "Didn't expect to hear from you, sweetheart."

"Thought I'd call before my afternoon patients arrive. Don't think I can pretend the sandwich I'm planning on eating for dinner is even half as good as your rack of lamb, though."

"Roast chicken tonight, actually."

His mouth watered. His mom had been making the savory, herb-forward dish for as long as he could remember. He'd tried his hand at it, but she put something into her cooking he could never replicate. "Sad to be missing it."

She paused. "Sad you don't have a table to sit at tonight."

"I'm not going to expire if I don't dip bread in salt on Fridays, Mom."

A gust of breath filled his ear. "It's about community, Caleb. The challah's just a vehicle."

Teenage Caleb deserved a slap up the back of the head for all the nights he'd spent wishing he could go out with his friends instead. Now that he could do whatever he wanted on Shabbat, gorging on roast chicken and arguing with his dad and brothers about the Islanders' chances at making the playoffs sounded just about perfect.

When he'd realized staying in Denver was holding him back from healing mentally, he'd had options. He could have just as easily moved back to Brooklyn instead of relocating to a town where he had all of two social connections. Maybe he should have.

But peaks and snow called to him, even if he missed surgery a thousand times more than he missed skiing.

Hell, he didn't miss going up mountains at all.

Or at least he'd keep telling himself that.

"Caleb, honey? Still there?"

"Yeah, sorry. Did I miss something you said?"

"No. But…" She sighed. "Promise me you won't eat alone tonight?"

A particularly godawful rendition of "All I Want for Christmas Is You" drifted in from the hallway through the door, open a hand crack. He kicked it shut with his foot and said, "I'll give Zach a call."

"You've been there for four months and Zach's still your only option?"

"No." Well, sort of. "Yesterday I had lunch with someone."

"A female someone?"

Damn, he should have known she'd want details. And Caleb had noticed far too many of Garnet James's details during their meal.

"Yeah, one of the local health practitioners."

"And her name?"

He nudged his glasses up to pinch the bridge of his nose. "Mom, stop. It was just a business lunch."

Another long breath threatened to burst his eardrum. "You don't function well without a big social circle."

He made a noncommittal noise. She was right, but admitting he was lonely would worry her way too much.

"You need to meet more people there," his mom said. "Have you looked into making connections with the search and rescue crew at all? You were so good at—"

"Mom. No way can my hand manage backcountry skiing." Just saying the word *backcountry* made his tongue feel thick in his mouth. And it was easier for Caleb to claim physical impairment than admit to the marrow-deep fear he'd failed to shed, despite his therapists' concerted efforts since the avalanche.

"No one's saying you need to go out in the field, Caleb. There are other ways to help out." His mom tsked. "You never know what'll work for you."

Yeah, like a pile of loose red curls and gray eyes that snapped like a flash storm. "I'm taking things one step at a time."

His mother made an unconvinced noise. "Some of the best things in life come when we take risks. You've proved that many times over."

Until it almost killed me. Throat muscles tensing, he coughed. "If I promise to go out for drinks when I leave the clinic, can we talk about something else?"

She agreed with an obvious pause, then filled him in on his niece's week at school, and his younger twin brothers' goings-on before signing off to finish her meal prep. By the time he finished up his afternoon appointments and the stack of paperwork he wanted off his desk before he left for the weekend, it was past seven. Knowing his mom was right about him needing to get out and socialize, he texted Zach to check if there was anything happening that night. A message reading Come to the hotel lounge arrived in seconds. Excellent. Should he go home, change out of his dress shirt and slacks? Nah. It wasn't a quick jaunt out and back to his lakeside house. But walking into the bustling space fifteen minutes later, he felt a little out of place. Despite the upscale decor, his button-down shirt shouted overdressed—most of the occupants were of the thermal-wear, après-ski variety. His glasses steamed up from the quick change from the outside cold to the indoor warmth. Untucking the tails of his shirt, he polished his foggy lenses.

The place was packed with people happy to swig beer

and watch a hockey game on the big screens mounted behind the long tin-topped bar. He spotted Zach and Cadie partway across the room, at the head of a six-person table currently seating a good ten.

Wading his way through the throng, he breathed slowly, bracing against the cacophony of sound. Loud noises bugged him since getting caught in the slide.

So sue him.

Nothing wrong with a few lingering symptoms. He was still going to counseling, even though his progress had stagnated some. Probably would have to learn to live with what was left, the same as learning to live with being a general practitioner instead of a surgeon. And for all that it wasn't surgery, his new position had its charms.

Or it will when you finally feel like you're making a difference.

With his oncologist father and dermatologist mother well versed in hospital politics, he'd been instructed not to get too big for his medical britches many a time. Surgeons got to walk around hospitals like rock stars. He didn't need that. Didn't need to be a star at all. Just needed to know he mattered, that he was still having an impact.

Skirting around one last table, he sidled up to Zach Cardenas, slapping the ski patrol director on the back and dropping a kiss on the cheek of Zach's girlfriend, Cadie. Other than Cadie, who wore jeans and a sweater, the rest of the crowded table had come straight from the hill and had stripped off half their layers. The damp-fabric-and-fresh-snow smell coming off their clothes was nostalgic as hell.

"You haven't joined us recently—do you still remember everyone?" Zach made cursory introductions of the handful of patrollers, and Lachlan Reid, a local veterinary technician and one of Zach's search and rescue buddies.

Zach waved a hand at a downright stunning woman to the left of Cadie. "And you know my sister."

"Hey, there," Marisol said, standing and leaning over the massive nacho platter to give him a hug. "Been a while."

"That it has." Since two days before the avalanche, actually. Zach's sister had met up with the film crew for drinks before the fatal trip into the Whistler backcountry. Caleb had been busy arguing on the phone with his girlfriend, Meiko, who hadn't appreciated him using his limited time off to work on ski documentaries. He hadn't spent much time with Marisol that night. Now, as he squeezed her back, he did a double take. If he'd ever wanted to know what Zach looked like in female form, there was his answer. Green eyes and light brown skin and a grin that lit up the room.

A lot like Garnet's had in the coffee shop.

Before he'd shot down her plans.

Guilt panged through his gut. Now that he'd confirmed he'd had no more luck than she at securing a venue in the village, would he have to admit he wouldn't be able to attend a party up the mountain? He could always claim illness the day of, salvage his pride.

"Here for a visit?" he asked, heading for the last empty seat and refocusing on Marisol.

"Yeah, until next Saturday."

"Welcome to Sutter Creek," he said. "Not that I've been here much longer than you."

"We'll make a local out of you yet." A feminine voice came from over his shoulder, stopping him mid-sit.

Echoes of that voice had been following him around since lunch yesterday. Figured he'd get a repeat of the real thing.

"And that's my spot," the voice continued.

"Garnet. Hi." He straightened, shifted around the chair and held it out for her. Sitting, she smiled. A waft of something herbal drifted from her pinned-up hair. The pretty smell went straight through his belly and a tense, hot knot gripped his core. He resisted the urge to lean in and nuzzle. A guy could spend hours playing with that perfect mess of curls…

No. That was not what he'd meant when he'd been thinking of making social connections. Going out for beers with the ski patrol was one thing. Actually being interested in one of them was another. His relationship with Meiko had been a casualty of the avalanche as much as his hand. He knew to avoid starting something up with someone whose ski-focused lifestyle mirrored that of his ex-girlfriend.

You were similar enough before the avalanche.

He gave himself a mental smack. Who he had been didn't matter. His life was what it was now, and he wasn't about to apologize for it.

Zach poured Caleb a beer from the communal pitcher, and Cadie perched on Zach's lap to make room for Caleb. Envy speared through him, and he covered it with a smile. Somehow, Zach and Cadie had managed to get through their own traumas without needing to turtle. Probably helped that Zach had been back at base camp instead of getting buried like Caleb. Didn't have to ask why he'd been pulled out and the others hadn't, or process the feelings that came from that. But still… Zach had dealt with survivor's guilt, and he and Cadie had mourned Cadie's husband's death and had fallen in love in the process. Caleb had done the opposite.

He settled next to Garnet and listened with half an ear as she, Cadie and Zach peppered Marisol with questions about what she labeled "her never-ending PhD course-work."

He took a few long drinks from his pint glass. This is what he'd been going for. Basic beer-on-a-Friday-night shenanigans.

"Came looking for me?" Garnet murmured, sipping what looked like a Bloody Mary. She wore leggings and a long plaid shirt-thing. A belt cinched her ribs, pulling the fabric tight to her breasts.

He swallowed, forcing himself to keep his eyes on her face instead of her just-right curves. "Not exactly."

"And did you manage to get any calls in?" she said lightly.

"Yep."

She shifted in her seat, and her arm brushed against him.

There was that knot again, tensing once, twice, just enough to remind him that the pheromones he learned about in premed biology could be a very real thing.

A smile danced on her lips, but unlike at the coffee shop, caution edged her demeanor. "Any success?"

"The Loose Moose is available."

"No effing way."

"It could be great," he said, hating the desperation in his voice.

"No. Ef—"

"Effing way, yeah, heard you the first time," he muttered. Pain shot up his right wrist and he glanced at it. Ah, damn. He was fisting his hand. Relaxing the muscles, he rubbed at one of the knots.

"Did you exhaust the list?"

"Maybe."

"You promised me an email."

"I'd planned to wait my full forty-eight hours before admitting you were right. Hope for a personal, pre-Hanukkah miracle."

A peal of laughter rang bright. "And here I was, doubting you had a sense of humor."

His stomach clenched. Hunger. Had to be that. Not disappointment that she clearly found him lacking. With a wordless point to the nachos that garnered a help-yourself wave from Cadie, he snagged a loaded chip and chewed, only catching half the flavor of cheese and salt.

"Want to meet up tomorrow? Keep planning?" she said.

He swallowed his bite. A random cramp pulsed along his forearm, and he failed to keep a grimace off his face. "Yeah, sure."

"I— Yesterday, you left suddenly. Sorry if I made you uncomfortable by bringing up alternative therapies." She bit her plump lower lip.

Well, that looks enjoyable.

No. It had beyond sucked to let Meiko down in the months following the slide. To not be the man she'd fallen in love with anymore. He'd changed too much, unable to participate in their usual daredevil pastimes. They hadn't had enough in common to make a relationship work anymore. And he wouldn't make that same mistake again.

Resisting the temptation to further contemplate Garnet's mouth—she didn't have gloss or lipstick on, which made it doubly hard to refocus, because damn, he loved the unadorned look—he nodded, accepting her excuse. Heat raced into his cheeks. Her suggesting acupressure had been fine. He'd been running away from how much he wanted to cancel his afternoon appointments to keep staring at her face. "I was just in a hurry to get back to work."

Her relief came out in a smile. "How much reconstruction did you need?"

"Too much." A muscle spasmed in his jaw to match the twinges in his hand, and he fought to keep his teeth from clenching. Apparently, she'd taken his acceptance as carte blanche to talk about the slide. He wasn't used to that. But something about her made his mouth start flapping again. "I had surgeries off and on for months after."

"Must've been weird, being the one on the table."

"At least I knew what to expect." Between the pain of having his hand crushed by debris and the terror of being under snow, the only way he'd kept himself from freaking out while buried had been to run through the surgeries he knew he was going to need. It had been calming, reverting to work.

And he hadn't effectively held a scalpel since.

"Such a fun conversation for a Friday night." He took a long drink from his beer and pretended to listen in on whatever conversation Zach was having with his sister across the table.

Garnet's eyes went a little bright, and her chest rose and fell, casting a shadow between her breasts. "Didn't mean to pry."

Stop noticing the neckline of her shirt, jackass. "Yeah, you did. And it's okay. People get weird about the slide, but it's easier when they don't pretend—"

"I never pretend to be something I'm not." Her hand tensed around her glass. "Not any—"

The abrupt halt to her words gave him pause. Everything about her, from her stiff posture to the flashing shards of silver in her eyes, warned him to pay attention.

"Anymore?" he finished softly.

"No." She shook her head. "I was going to say, uh, not in any world."

He'd give her that lie. Seemed the truth would cost her. She cleared her throat. "I'm surprised that you've tried acupressure. A lot of doctors are still on the fence when it comes to energy treatments. Then again, with you being—"

"Part Japanese?" he said, saying it before she did. Being biracial meant he got a lot of stupid questions. Sometimes it was easier to cut things off at the pass. "Must be into Shiatsu and finding my qi?"

Her mouth fell open and she reddened. "No. Zach said you were progressive as a surgeon and might be interested in holistic treatments."

He winced. Not at the misread, but at the reminder that his reputation had preceded him. Man, he'd hoped to leave reminders of what he'd lost back in Denver. "I was. And I have no problem referring people who are open to alternative therapy, Garnet. Some of the woo-woo stuff is a bit much for me, but I can usually see the science behind it."

"Woo-woo?" She leaned in, close enough for him to catch another delicious wave of rosemary off her hair. "I get science, Caleb. Half a master's in biochem even gives me partial street cred. But some things can't be explained in a lab."

A thrill of challenge skimmed his skin. Goddamn, she pushed his buttons.

"Is that so?" he said, for her ears only. He wanted to hear more of that purring promise in her voice. Except about non-work-related things. "I'm not easily convinced."

"I'd be happy to try."

Chapter Four

Confusion tumbled through Garnet's stomach. After his skepticism, she was supposed to be annoyed, not flirting with him. But the minute she'd heard his voice crack when he'd mentioned no longer performing surgery, her empathetic side, already on alert after talking with Cadie and Lauren, had roared to full capacity. His monumental recovery had hit her right in her soft parts.

The way his eyes went vulnerable behind his sexy, geeky glasses...

I'd be happy to try?

Where the hell had that come from? Ugh, she was so crappy at nuance. Growing up an only child had done her no favors socially. Nor had being raised by two professors who were more comfortable researching nanotechnology than they were talking about things so basic as flirting.

Or not flirting. Stop. Flirting. With. Him.

"Caleb?" Zach's sister broke into the conversation. "Zach's been terrible at keeping me up to date—have you and Meiko both moved here?"

Caleb's unscarred hand flattened on the small table. "Uh, no. We broke things off a while back."

With a sympathetic expression, Marisol reached over and covered his hand with hers. "So sorry to hear that."

Yeah, right. Garnet gritted her teeth to stop herself from laughing in disbelief.

Caleb shrugged and drained his beer with his free

hand, not bothering to move the one that Marisol was squeezing.

She could let go anytime now.

Ugh, *why do I care?*

Because the two seconds he had his hand over hers at lunch yesterday had been the freaking highlight of her week.

"You didn't come back to film the reunion tape," Marisol commented, finally releasing Caleb's hand.

His complexion turned a little green at the mention of the memorial film Zach and the other survivors had created to honor the avalanche victims. Garnet hadn't realized Caleb hadn't participated. *Interesting.*

He busied himself pouring another beer, then slamming back half of it. "Yeah, well, work didn't allow it when Zach went up."

Their tablemates' shifting gazes made it obvious no one else was as insensitive as Garnet had been when she'd asked about his avalanche experience. Caleb might have claimed he preferred it when people didn't coddle him, but he'd probably just said that to be kind. Shame burned her cheeks.

Nodding and changing the subject, Marisol made a joke about the New York Islanders that had Caleb laughing but made absolutely no sense to Garnet.

A wash of being entirely out of place swept over her.

She picked at the hem of her plaid tunic, wishing for some frame of reference—hockey, yeah, they were still talking about hockey. One of her ex-boyfriends had been a Minnesota Wild fan, so naturally she'd also started following the team for a few months, and…

And *blech*, she had really sucked in college. She'd also gone through stints of loving ballroom dancing, stock-car racing, eating vegan, listening exclusively to Baroque music—whatever the guy she'd been dating had loved, she'd loved it, too. And yeah, trying new things wasn't wrong, but when she did so at the expense of the things she actually loved in life? Not healthy. She'd spent the five years since quitting grad school figuring out what *she* loved. And she wasn't giving up that progress.

It was easier to avoid relationships than risk sliding back into being that wishy-washy woman again.

Flirtatious laughter broke into Garnet's thoughts as Marisol reached across the table and playfully swatted Caleb's wrist. "At least your team made it into the play-offs in the past few years," Marisol grumbled.

Was Caleb into the playful attention? Garnet couldn't tell. He had that neutral expression of his on. Very emergency room-ish of him. He'd probably trained himself to catalog everything about a situation without ever letting on to what he was thinking.

"Figures you'd be into hockey, being from Canada," Garnet blurted when Marisol laughed again.

Oh, frick. Talk about rude.

Marisol's generous smile turned wooden, and the others at the table, including a few 'trollers, looked at Garnet like her hair had turned to snakes. By the fact she could feel her skin crawling on her neck, there was a possibility it had.

"You know us Canadians," the other woman said carefully. "Ever the clichés."

"I'm so sorry," Garnet said, closing her eyes. Even with her lids blocking out the world, the weight of her friends' stares was heavy on her skin. She opened her eyes and faced Marisol straight on. "I was—" *Insecure...jealous...* "Thinking about something else and not watching my tone. That came out wrong."

An arm slid along the back of her chair. Not quite around her shoulders. Close enough, though.

She shouldn't want it there. When was the closed-off, bolting-from-the-coffee-shop guy from earlier going to come back?

"Garnet just feels sorry for you that you cheer for Vancouver," he said. A bit of a Brooklyn accent marred the low, smooth tone.

Marisol's gaze landed on the position of Caleb's arm. A knowing light dawned in her green eyes and she nodded. "*I* feel sorry for me that I cheer for Vancouver. It's painful at times."

The conversation drifted to other things. Cadie and Zach sloughed off probing questions about when they were getting engaged. The two of them looked like they'd be happier if they were attached with Velcro, though they were doing a good job of trying to replicate that with Cadie snuggled on Zach's lap.

How nice would that be, spending the evening cozied up in someone's embrace?

Oof. That was not a fantasy she could afford to dwell on. But the silent assumptions Marisol had made when Caleb had put his arm around Garnet? Garnet couldn't quite bring herself to correct the other woman.

Nor could she bring herself to nudge his arm away.

A few hours later, Caleb braced his hands on the pool table and watched Garnet methodically annihilate Zach. His friend was holding his own a little better than Caleb had—given his awkward grip on his cue, she'd managed to beat him in five shots—but the striped balls still outnumbered the solids three to one on the table.

"Four in the side pocket," she called, then tapped in the purple ball with ease.

Zach scowled good-heartedly. "You're no fun, James."

She straightened and sighed. "Sorry. Do you want me to lose? I could try."

"Hell, no," Zach said as she lined up to sink the eight ball. "Either way, my pride's demolished."

The ball landed in the pocket with a soft thunk, and an apologetic look crossed Garnet's face. She hadn't acted nearly so sorry when she'd beaten Caleb.

Her competitive streak was so damn adorable. Made him want to find a game they could play where he'd have half a chance of beating her, so he could actually give her a real challenge.

"Aw, Zach," Marisol razzed from her perch on a nearby barstool. She had been deep in conversation with Lachlan Reid during Garnet's reign over the pool table. "You didn't hear Caleb complaining about his masculinity."

He caught Garnet's gaze. A hint of interest there, quickly covered by irritation. And a little bit more sympathy than he liked. He preferred her earlier grilling of him.

"You need to feel like a man, Zach? I have some ideas," Cadie said, sidling up to her boyfriend with her beer bottle dangling between her fingers.

He pointed at her with his cue. "Now we're talking." He turned to Marisol. "Want a ride home? Or are you going to cab it later?"

She whispered something to Lachlan, who nodded, his eyes brightening. Drawing a circle in the air to frame her brother and his girlfriend, she said, "Go home to your adorable kid and ratty-sweatpants domesticity. Lachlan and I are going to catch a late movie. I'll let myself in."

Zach sized up the vet tech for a second, then shrugged and handed Caleb his pool cue. "Your turn again. See if you can gather up the remaining dregs of your ego."

The two couples said their goodbyes and headed for

the door, Zach and Cadie with that close ease of an established couple, Marisol and Lachlan with the curious spark of two people who were sizing each other up.

Garnet went to put her cue back on the wall rack, but Caleb covered the slot with his hand. He didn't want to go home yet. It had been way too long since he'd stayed up until midnight for reasons other than his overnight on-call shift at the Sutter Creek hospital. "Teach me your tricks, Sharky."

Her eyes widened, glinting in the lights hanging over the pool table. "I—I don't know what to tell you. I just have a knack with physics." She motioned up and down at his body, then hers. "And it's not like I could spoon you and show you how to hold the cue or anything—you're too tall." She reddened and coughed. "That's not what you meant, was it?"

His brain stuttered at the suggestion of her sexy body plastered against his, guiding him to make a shot. "I'm not hitting on you, Garnet. I just don't feel like going home yet."

Relief tinged her smile. "I wasn't sure. We were almost flirting earlier, and then you put your arm on my chair. I didn't know what to think."

"I was thinking you needed a save." Nothing beyond that. He needed to look for someone more in line with his newfound nine-to-five-and-don't-take-chances mentality.

She cleared her throat. "And the flirting?"

"I just want to play pool, Garnet." When she didn't lose her uncertain expression, he tossed a little more honesty. "And to make a few friends. That hasn't come quite as easy as I expected." Hard when most everyone in town spent their spare time on the mountain.

"Not surprising, given you use descriptors like 'woo-woo' in reference to others' jobs."

He opened his mouth, then closed it when no reasonable defense came to mind.

"Yeah, thought so." She clicked her cue back on the wall rack.

"Wait," he said. "I'm sorry for how I worded that. It was insulting and unprofessional. But do we need to be ideologically aligned to play another game of pool?"

Why was he pushing so hard? If she didn't want to associate with him outside of work, so be it.

But she was interesting, and his life had lacked that since he accepted he wouldn't be getting on skis again anytime soon, if ever. No way should he consider anything beyond friendship with her. Though it was Friday, and he really liked seeing her smile. She'd made *him* smile. More than he had in a while. Maybe some innocent flirting was exactly what was needed here.

"We could up the ante if you like," he suggested.

"How so?" Lifting an auburn brow, she took her cue down again and chalked it.

"A bet of some kind." He chalked his own cue and started racking the balls.

Sighing, she nudged him aside and took over, jolting the rack with precision. She motioned to the cue ball. "You break. What are we playing for?"

"How about whoever loses gets to pick the menu for the party?"

She shook her head, and a sexy tendril fell from her up-do and fluttered to her jawline. She brushed it behind her ear. "No way. Not good enough."

A shiver ran up his spine. "The Peak Lounge can't be the prize, Garnet."

"I know. I wasn't going to ask that." Damn, her sympathy was edging into full-on pity.

A dark frustration ate at his gut. "No, you know what?

That's perfect. The venue it is. Peak Lounge if you win, Loose Moose if I do."

He waved at a waiter, pointed at his beer and held up two fingers, then got to work.

Garnet eyed the ball-scattered table and mentally played ahead a few moves. Not an exact science, of course, but like she'd told Caleb, she had a knack for physics, and was usually able to predict where the cue ball would end up. He'd sunk two balls before scratching, meaning Garnet had some catching up to do.

He'd apologized for the "woo-woo" comment. Simple, to the point, actually expressing regret for what he'd said and not some crappy "sorry your feelings got hurt" type of runaround. She'd been surprised.

She *hadn't* been surprised when she'd opened her big mouth and made that asinine comment about spooning. God, she could slap herself sometimes, the way things ended up coming out.

His mouth quirked, framed by a dark five o'clock shadow. "Gonna take your turn sometime before New Year's?"

"Pool shark lesson number one—patience."

With his cue resting on the edge of the table and his unscarred hand splayed on the wood, his forearm muscles stood out in impressive relief. He'd rolled up his sleeves before his turn. *Mmm.* Something about a turned-up cuff made Garnet's knees shaky. Like at the coffee shop, he was a little overdressed, but he sure as hell wore it well. Crisp cotton over broad shoulders. His dress pants advertised the fact he had an ass that didn't quit.

He coughed. "Is lesson number two to stare at your opponent to throw off his technique?"

Heat rushed into her cheeks at having been caught

checking him out instead of paying attention to the lie of the balls. "Um, obviously. It's a two-fold lesson. Gotta check your opponent out for weaknesses—" of which he seemed to have none, the jerk "—and play mind games at the same time."

Or imagine him unbuttoning more than just the cuffs of his shirt. That could work, too.

She lined up her first shot, a cut shot to a corner pocket, followed by a combo that sank one ball in each of the side pockets.

"We're even," she said.

Caleb slowly shook his head. "Like I said—Sharky."

"I'll wear the title. Earn it by winning, in fact."

You sure about that? What if he actually has PTSD? Then you're going to feel like a jerk.

He eyed her, as if reading her doubt. "Do not hold back on me. If you're going to win, win."

The permission didn't calm her churning gut. If his losing meant more than just a pool game to him…

"Don't," he murmured.

Fine. She wouldn't throw her shot. Taking a centering breath, she leaned over the table to line up, and he sidled close, resting his hands on the table a few inches from her cue stick. "Talk me through what you're doing. I'm trying to learn here."

"I'm going to put spin on it to make the rail shot. English. Uh, side spin."

She drew back and took the shot just as he said, "Damn, it's hot when you get technical like that."

A sheer sexual growl roughened his voice. She jolted, screwing up her aim. The cue ball spun too hard, sending the purple four ball careening off the rail.

She straightened, glaring at him. "You did that on purpose."

He smirked.

"Literally dirty pool, Dr. Matsuda."

Lifting a shoulder, he took his turn, sinking one ball and then entirely missing on the next.

"I hope you're a better doctor than you are a pool strategist."

The corners of his mouth fell.

She paused, wariness poking at her consciousness. "I…"

With a long blink, he recovered. He smiled, the set of his lips stiff. "One would indeed hope."

Feeling chastened, she stared at the table and sank two balls in short order. God, why had she said that? Of course he'd be sensitive about his job. She closed her eyes briefly. Fricking mouth, going off without permission. "I didn't mean…"

"Shark lesson number three, right? Trash talking?" He smiled again, smaller this time, but a little less forced. Stiff fingers holding his cue, he reached toward her with his free hand, brushing a roughened thumb down her cheek.

A shiver spread from her face through her chest. Oh. Well, then. "Are you left-handed? You have calluses."

Wow. Her tongue was really on fire tonight. She swore under her breath.

Warmth glinted in his deep brown eyes. "No, I've had to compensate for all the time I wasn't able to use my right. And I kayak and canoe for as much of the year as I can. You know how it is."

"Sure, yeah. Is that why you bought a place out on the lake?"

He raised his eyebrows.

"Small town, Caleb. Everyone knows everything about everyone. You'll be gossip fodder for a good few months yet," she mused. Or until one of the nurses at the clinic coaxed him into a diamond solitaire and a minivan with two car seats. Apparently, there was a betting pool going on as to who would nab him first. She'd stayed far away from those conversations. Until she figured out how to function in a relationship without losing herself, marriage and babies were not in the cards.

A shadow crossed his handsome face. "Everything, huh?"

"*Almost* everything," she amended. Though he'd probably be aghast at how much the gossip chain was able to figure out just by guessing.

"Almost," he echoed, voice a rasp. He cleared his throat. "You going to finish me off, or will I get another turn?"

"Are you going to cheat again?"

He shook his head.

Disappointment flashed for a second, which was ridiculous. She needed to win this game, not to get distracted by strategic flirting. "Then yeah, I shouldn't need more than this turn."

"Okay," he said evenly. "And I want step-by-step explanations for how you're going to annihilate me."

She explained a combo shot to him, sinking her last two solids, and the impressed look he bestowed on her warmed her straight through.

"How'd you get so good at pool?"

Because my high school boyfriend had a table in his basement and I feigned interest in everything he loved.

"Practice." Lining up to sink the eight ball, she called her pocket and drew back. "If you talk during my shot, I may kill you."

"Kiss me?"

Her stomach tightened. Yeah, that sounded good.

Those lips of his looked pretty much made for that very act. "No, kill you."

"But there's mistletoe above your head."

She struck the cue ball way too hard. The eight ball sank, sure, but in the far corner pocket, not the side like she'd called it.

She swore, and looked up. Someone had dangled mistletoe from fishing line at various points around the room. *Subtle, lounge staff, really subtle.* "I lost because of effing mistletoe?"

"No, you lost because I was being an asshole, distracting you on purpose." His soft smile vanished. "I'd say I owe you that venue, fair and square."

"Caleb, I want the Peak Lounge, but I can't feel right about forcing it on you," she whispered.

His hand tightened on his cue. "You're not."

"Are you sure?"

"*Yes.* Don't compromise for me."

Normally she'd love hearing that from a guy. But God, he had a good reason for his reluctance… "Want to meet up for coffee tomorrow? Get some more planning done? Does four o'clock sound okay?"

"Yeah, great." Face a shade paler than normal, he glanced up at the offending sprig. "Tradition would suggest a kiss."

Her pulse leaped. What? He couldn't seriously mean… His mouth twitched, curiosity, not humor, and she scrambled for a subject change. "Do you even observe Christmas traditions?"

Oh, religion. Nice, nonawkward conversational choice. Good grief.

He rubbed the back of his neck. "My dad's a lapsed Methodist, so we celebrate Christmas with his family.

How about you? Is your—" he cleared his throat "—your training a spiritual thing, or just for medical purposes?"

"Mostly medical. I was raised by two scientists—not a lot of room for theology there. But I do have some theories about cells and energy that you'd probably classify as—" she raised her finger to make air quotes, and he beat her to the phrase.

"'Woo-woo,' yeah, I know." He reddened, glancing up at the mistletoe again.

"Not a good idea."

"Not good, or not smart?" He hitched a hip on the table a few inches from her. Holy crackers, he smelled fantastic. Clean, a little spicy. Warm. Lickable.

Entirely good.

But entirely wrong. "Not smart."

"Fair." A *what the hell was I thinking?* look crossed his face. "Should we play another game, or call it a night?"

"I have a morning patrol shift, so I'd better get home and hit the sack."

The warmth in his eyes faded. "Patrol. Right."

"You take issue with ski patrol? Jesus, my parents would love you." Her ex-boyfriend would have, too, at least later in their relationship. Bryce hadn't started out by telling her she should give up her job on the mountain. It had been little things. *Can't you switch your shift, Garnet? There's a graduate student mixer.* And then: *You really should be focusing on your lab research instead of goofing around on the mountain.*

Or her personal favorite: *Don't you know how embarrassing it was to explain to my parents that you're a ski bum?*

Adam's apple bobbing, Caleb shook his head. "I admire anyone who's willing to work in emergency services, Garnet. Promise."

She nodded. The healer inside her urged her to find a gentle way to ask him about the mental scars from the avalanche, but her gut was insistent that she needed to be careful. With his feelings, and her own. His wariness of her being on ski patrol hit a still-raw nerve. She did not need another man making her question herself or feel like she was less. For the sake of Evolve's success and partnership with the clinic, she'd work with him to plan a banging party. And then she'd keep her distance. She could change all she wanted, but she still had hella bad taste in guys.

Chapter Five

Caleb walked into Peak Beans on Saturday afternoon at four on the dot, hoping the headache that painkillers refused to kill wasn't showing on his face. Garnet was already at the pickup counter, chatting with the barista and holding two large to-go cups in her mittened hands.

He sidled up to her. "Hey. If that's for me, you didn't have to."

"I know. My treat, though." Going by her wind-nipped cheeks, she hadn't arrived that long ago. Her hair, pulled back into a braid and mostly covered with a floppy dark green knitted hat, looked pure auburn. But he'd stared at it enough while they were playing pool last night to know strands of strawberry gold were hiding somewhere, just waiting to catch the light. Her brows crinkled. "What's wrong?"

"Nothing." The word came out sharper than he'd intended. "Looking forward to firming up plans."

She passed him his drink and steered him toward the door. "No way. You're not feeling well. Here, let's get outside."

He took a deep breath of twilight air. A cold sting pinched his lungs. He took a seat at one of the cafe tables arranged on the edge of the raised wood-planked walkway that edged the pedestrian-dominated town center.

"Better?" she asked.

"I'm not nauseated. It's just a headache." Came on

today after he'd tried to visualize going up the gondola to the Peak Lounge and failing hard. He had a raft of centering and anchoring techniques from his therapist, but they hadn't worked today. "Hard to keep the memories at bay, sometimes."

"Well, why didn't you say so? If you want, I can help with the headache." Garnet's mouth firmed in determination, and regret rolled through Caleb's stomach. He'd admitted too much. It wasn't his intention to hide his PTSD, exactly. Impossible to go from being a skier who attacked some of the toughest backcountry conditions to not even bringing his equipment when he moved from Colorado without anyone noticing. But he didn't make a habit of announcing his fears in the middle of the town square, either.

"What, you want to treat me?" he said.

"If you want to give it a try. Let's skip planning today. We'll walk over to Evolve, and I'll see what I can do for your headache. Then we can come back here—the tree lighting's at five thirty, and pretty much the whole town attends. If you're interested."

"I am." In getting rid of his headache, and in joining her friends for another evening.

"Okay, then follow me." Ten minutes later, she had him stripped out of his winter coat and stationed on his back on a treatment table in a low-lit room. "Here, smell this."

She wafted a bottle under his nose and he inhaled. Lavender and something else. Another deep breath, and the pain in his head eased a degree.

"I'm going to work on your head and face, and then your hands and arms."

He nodded, trying to relax as she pressed at a muscle in his shoulder. "That's not quite my head, Garnet."

"Mmm." She kept pressing the spot.

Good thing she had music on. The classical cello accompaniment helped him to avoid the spiral of silence that had threatened to suck him under while he'd tried to meditate at home. So he focused on her hands, on her touch. The warmth of her fingers bled through his sweater. And when she laid a second hand on him, a firm pressure on his forearm, he felt his muscles shift. The palm of his hand tingled. She must have hit a point that loosened the fascial tissue in his arm.

Or he just liked having her hands on him.

Her warm herbal scent floated over him and his breath hitched. Yeah, there was definitely some truth to his second theory. He glanced at her face. A soft, dreamy smile graced her pretty mouth.

Her mouth probably tasted as good as the rest of her smelled.

She released his arm and shoulder and switched to the other side of the table, repeating the pressure in the same places. The same thing happened—when she applied her finger to his forearm, a tangible shift occurred.

"You're probably going to tell me it's like connecting a circuit, aren't you?" he said.

Her quiet laugh surprised him.

"No?"

"No. It's not like a current, Caleb. Energy doesn't move from me to you. The theory is that your energy responds to mine."

Oh, he was responding to her, all right. Not his energy, but other parts of him.

She shifted to up near his head, manipulating points behind his ears.

He damned near moaned. "That's just unfair. Trying to woo me with a scalp massage?"

"Shh. To get anything out of this, you need to relax.

Focus on my fingers and let your body do what it needs to do to let go of your tension."

God, her touch was perfect, the exact balance between gentle and firm on the muscles of his skull. She slid her fingers behind his neck finding mirrored points. Tense mirrored points. Ouch.

"Breathe, Caleb."

He followed instructions, inhaling a lungful of her soothing perfume. And a hint of raspberries, too. Her lips were pink—did she have on flavored gloss? Seemed like a good idea to test it out—

"Keep doing whatever you're doing," she murmured. "Your muscles are liking it."

He groaned inwardly. More thoughts of testing her lips, her skin, for the taste of sweet fruit and he'd slide right into dangerous territory. He switched mental gears to doing times tables. The last thing he wanted was to tent his jeans, for crying out loud.

She tended to points around his temples and eyes, which he kept closed. Keeping his breath shallow, he tolerated her ministrations for a few more minutes.

She ended with a finger pressed between his brows. Warmth spread out from the point, and his hands tingled again.

Weird.

"There," she said. "Better. You tensed up again for a bit."

"Sorry."

"This is about you, not me." She withdrew her hand and a second later he heard a chair creak. "How's your headache?"

"It's feeling okay."

"Good. And the rest of you?"

There but for the grace of some quick multiplication

recitation, he would have been embarrassed as anything, but thankfully, Mrs. Barnes of P.S. 29 had drilled that sucker into him for the entirety of fourth grade. Without having to worry about the state of his groin, he was free to take stock of the rest of his body. Which felt pretty light, actually. "I'm as relaxed as anyone would be after getting to chill on a comfy table for half an hour."

"You fought it, though."

I fought wanting you, not the treatment. Shrugging, he sat up, a rush of blood going to his head. *Whoa.* He gripped the edge of the table.

She studied him with knitted brows, and stood. Taking his right hand, she pressed into a point on his arm above his wrist.

"I'm fine," he murmured. He covered her hand with his. "Treatment's over."

She stopped pressing, but didn't take her hand away. Her fingers drifted along the base of his scarred palm. "You seemed dizzy."

"I was."

"Does that happen to you a lot?"

"A lot? No." And usually only when he was dealing with anxiety. This spurt of unsteadiness had nothing to do with his PTSD and everything to do with the fact she'd had her hands on his face. Strangely intimate, that. So was having her hand in such proximity to his. He closed the gap, trapping her fingers with his.

"But sometimes," she prodded.

"Nothing I can't handle."

Her hand tightened around his. "Caleb, you shouldn't have to 'handle' anything, especially not the effects of trauma."

He caught her chin with his thumb and forefinger. "Don't worry about me, Sharky."

Her eyes filled with concern. And he'd put that look there. Her lips parted, and a hint of heat warmed the unhappy gray of her gaze.

Huh. He'd hazard a guess that he put that look there, too. And maybe he could get rid of her displeasure entirely... He leaned forward a fraction, honing in on her plush mouth.

She jolted back, yanking her hand away and breaking their eye contact. Backing toward the door, she dragged a hand over her face. "My treatment room—I shouldn't... I mean..."

He cringed. He couldn't deny he felt pretty loose right now, and her fingers had eased his headache as well as pain relievers—but that didn't excuse him being unprofessional in her workspace. Nor was Garnet the right person to be casually involved with. Between their professional ties and their shared friends, kissing her would be a mistake and a half.

"Let's head to the tree lighting, then."

Winter chill numbed the tip of his nose as they walked the block back to the town square. A few flakes drifted from the black sky. No stars framed the mountain peaks. But the town made up for the lack of stellar scenery. Thick evergreen swags, dotted with white lights and draped at even intervals from one side of the street to the other, reminded Caleb of the winding brick roads in a Bavarian town he'd visited in college. Clusters of silver bells hung at the apex of each swath. A crowd milled around what had been a grassy expanse back in the fall.

She motioned toward a long table manned by a group of teenagers wearing Sutter Mountain Ski Club coats. "Apple cider?"

"Sure." He brushed a fat snowflake from the edge of her hat. It took a lot of effort not to trace his fingers down her jaw. Not that he would have been able to feel her soft skin through his fleece gloves, but something about her made him want to touch her regardless. "Lead the way."

Tugging him along by his elbow, in under a minute she had him clutching a hot apple cider and a gingerbread cookie. Her hands were full, too, so she was no longer holding his elbow.

And feeling even a little disappointed over that is too much. Dial it down. She's not for you.

People were clumped in irregular groups around a meters-high spruce tree that looked like it might be cultivated specifically for the purpose of being lit up.

"There's the gang over there." She motioned with her own cookie-holding hand. "Want to join them?"

"Of course." Hopefully, with a little more effort he'd be included in the "gang" category.

Though the prospect of being alone with her again tempted him equally.

Silently repeating that she wasn't for him, he took a drink from his cider and followed as she weaved through the crowd. Lots of families out and about—a few he recognized from the clinic and exchanged waves with. As they approached their friends, he narrowed his eyes.

Zach had an arm around Cadie and held Cadie's son in the other. Lauren Dawson was safely ensconced in the embrace of her fiancé, Tavish. Even Marisol and Lachlan Reid were all snuggly, talking to a strawberry-blond-haired woman who, by her brown eyes and crooked smile, had to be related to Lachlan. She held the leash of a golden retriever wearing a service vest.

Crap. This was super date-like. Full-on couple stuff.

Would that be so bad?

He jammed the rest of the cookie in his mouth and

chewed furiously, trying to prevent himself from answering the question with anything other than a fervent *yes*.

It wouldn't do him any good to entertain cuddling up with Garnet like the others were doing, no matter how much he'd like to loop his arms around her as they watched the show. He wasn't going to start a relationship with someone if there was no hope of longevity, and given how his neck sweated at the mere thought of strapping on skis, he didn't see how he could date someone who lived to carve up a slope. Who probably regularly went out on avalanche control as part of ski patrol.

Dread trickled down his neck, a cold drip of fear.

"Hey, everyone!" Garnet called, catching his elbow again and ushering him into the group. "T minus five minutes until tree time?"

"Around that," Cadie replied as the rest of the gathering called out their greetings. He didn't have more than a few seconds to smile back and return the hellos before Cadie fixed him with a pointed look. "Garnet said you were trying to secure a different place for the party. How's that going? The bookings manager says he can only hold the spot at the Peak Lounge until tomorrow."

"I thought Garnet and I had agreed that's what we'd book." He couldn't stop himself from frowning, so he hid it behind his cider cup. Arguing with Garnet about the location was one thing. Being a pain in the ass with Cadie, though? Zach was eyeing him funny, too… He couldn't complicate the few social ties he had over a party.

Regret shadowed Cadie's expression, and she looked like she was on the verge of apologizing.

Well, hadn't taken his friends long to figure out his weaknesses.

"It'll be fun," he lied.

Cadie's smile straddled soft and wary. Her son reached

out from Zach's arms to bat at the fluffy pom-pom on her hat. "I'll pay the deposit then," she said.

He swallowed against his tightening throat. "We'll make sure the expenses get split evenly between our clinic and yours."

"Yes, we'll— Oh, Ben!" Cadie exclaimed, turning her attention to her toddler. "Watch the tree, sweetie!"

"Hey," Garnet said softly. Her hand slid in Caleb's.

He let her see his surprise at the PDA.

She shrugged. "No one's looking."

"But we—"

"You looked like you needed it," she interrupted, voice still low. "Is it the skiing that's the problem? Or the mountain in general?"

Hell, what was the point in hiding? She had him beyond figured out. "Both. I thought moving here, facing it, would help. But nope."

She let out a sympathetic "Oh." The scent of apples and cinnamon rode her breath. Damn, she'd taste good—

"So what do you want to do?" she prodded.

"I'll help you plan the party."

"But how will you go?"

A gust of wind swirled around them, seeping under the collar of his coat. He squeezed her hand. "I won't."

The corners of her mouth turned down. "Caleb…"

"Don't worry about—"

Color flashed across Garnet's face as the strings of lights came to life. Her gray eyes caught flecks of blue and green, and a sad frown marred her expression as she peered over the crowd at the high school band, who launched into a rousing carol involving one too many sets of sleigh bells. "Oh… I missed it."

"I'm sorry. I distracted you."

She palmed his cheek, the fine wool of her glove soft against his skin. "No worries. I've seen it before."

Yikes, when was the last time he'd felt the urge to close his eyes and lean into someone's touch?

He exhaled the impulse. "You, uh, grew up here, right?"

"Between here and Bozeman. But I've worked for the mountain since I was a teenager. Except when—" Closing her eyes, she shook her head. "Well, it doesn't matter."

"You sure about that?"

She crossed her arms. "Are you trying to avoid talking about the party?"

His face heated, despite the cold air. Easier to admit to that than the degree to which he wished she was touching him again. He lifted a shoulder.

"Why don't you practice?" she blurted.

"Practice? What do you mean?"

Going on her toes, she leaned in close to his ear, presumably so she wouldn't have to shout over the damn sleigh bells, which had now been joined by cymbals. The band was dedicated to bringing the joy to "Joy to the World," all right. "Come up the mountain before the party. Join me for lunch or something."

Or something.

That was one way of putting it. Just *something* necessitating he ride a lift to get there.

Chest tightening, he wiggled his jaw, trying to keep the blood from draining out of his face. Ridiculous, really, that he had baggage around riding a chair up a mountain. The avalanche had happened in the British Columbia backcountry, miles away from any lifts. But much to his dismay, the human brain didn't always make sense. It was supposed to. Synapses and dendrites and connections and lovely, comforting science.

Science seemed to be failing him on this one, though.

"Or not…if you aren't ready…" Garnet's somber concern broke through his fear. She linked her fingers with his again.

A firm hand landed on his shoulder. Zach's. "You okay, Matsuda?"

He straightened. His friend was regarding him with the eye of a person who'd evaluated many an injured skier over the years. He bristled at the attention. He wasn't some wounded animal to be wary of. "Yeah, of course." He took a sip of his drink. "You should get some cider. Delicious."

"You were shaking. And you're a little gray," Zach said.

"Garnet and I were just discussing lunch up the mountain. No big deal."

Zach's gaze traveled from Caleb's face to Caleb and Garnet's clasped hands and back. "Like, midstation?"

Frustration burned behind Caleb's sternum. Good grief, what was with the people in his life and their doubt problems? He was freaking sick of it.

So prove them wrong.

"Yeah, midstation. Garnet, when are you patrolling this week?"

Her eyes widened. "Monday, Tuesday, Thursday."

"I'm off during the day on Monday." That would give him two days to brush up on the grounding techniques his therapist recommended he use. "I'll see you at the top of the quad chair whenever your lunch break starts."

"You sure?" she said, wariness riding her tone.

"It's a date."

Chapter Six

This is small.

No big deal.

Two days later, as he was standing in the walk-on line to head up the quad chair—no freaking way was he going up on skis—his brain faithfully recited the calming words.

His gut rejected them. Threatened to reject his breakfast, too.

Stop. It's just a chairlift.

Caleb had had twenty months to learn to deal with this, for God's sake. He wasn't going to get buried under snow while riding up the side of a hill. Nor was there any chance of it happening walking from the lift to the midstation Creekview Lodge. And especially not sitting on the lodge's deck, with the winter sun beating down on them.

Though it had been sunny the day of the slide.

And now the cool winter-white light pinched his retinas, even through his sunglasses. At least he had time to calm the hell down. He'd get up the hill and get his breathing under control before Garnet ever saw him.

His pride demanded the cover-up more than anything. She made a good ski patroller for a reason. Her chill demeanor and dry sense of humor—emergency personnel needed that on the hill, and then off it, too. He'd have to ask her which job she considered her primary occupation, if she was patrolling with the aim of building her acupressure practice on the side, or if she stuck with patrolling to get the free ski pass. She wouldn't be patrolling for the paycheck, that's for sure—the pay was abysmal.

The quad express hummed behind him, the vibration crawling on his skin. The cables and towers bisected a reasonably steep slope. A number of skiers dotted the white face, making their way down at various speeds.

A red jacket, a patroller's uniform, caught his attention. He'd expect a professional to make those smooth S turns with skis, but that didn't make it any less enthralling to watch.

Or to feel, to experience.

This time of year, skis cut into snow like a knife into butter. The perfect swoosh.

Heart panging with something way too close to yearning, he stared at the laces on his winter boots. Boots not attached to skis like those of everyone else in the lineup. Damn it. He stuck out like a hunk of metal on an X-ray slide.

It wasn't like no one ever rode up without intending to ski or board down—it was common enough that he'd been able to buy a discounted pass to get up the hill— but it was the first time he'd ever done it, and it grated.

The snick of ski edges rasping snow sounded in his ears. "Hey, doc, wanna skip the line? I hear you have a date to meet."

He looked up. A black helmet framed Garnet's face, hiding her vibrant hair from the world. She lifted her goggles onto the front of the protective shell. She wore a red jacket—obviously, she'd been the skier he'd been admiring. A feeling edging on lust tugged at his gut. Damn, she was sexy. He tried to cover his nerves with a cocky grin. "A date, huh?"

Her cheeks flushed beyond their already healthy, outdoor-air rose pink. "Your words."

He didn't mind that. In fact, he liked the idea of her knowing he was interested. She was the last woman he should be drawn to, but hell, maybe she'd be good for him. Maybe he'd been wrong about avoiding women who loved all the things he'd used to be able to love. Maybe to feel whole again, he needed to stop lurking on the edges of his preslide life. And Garnet seemed to be a good person to come out of the shadows for. Those gray eyes—a guy could spend a lot of time watching them sparkle in the sunshine.

Tugging at her lower lip with her teeth, she held up the line's rope for him to duck under. "We can skip to the front."

Wait, what? But he'd planned on using the wait time to center himself, to make sure all his nerves were invisible... Crap. He'd have to fake it. "Lead the way."

He followed her to the start of the line. His stomach churned, deeply unhappy about both life and the fried egg sandwich he'd had for breakfast.

Okay. Find an anchor... *Numbers on the chairs, Caleb. Numbers on the chairs.*

One forty-three.

One forty-four.

One forty-five.

That'd be the one they'd sit on.

One forty-five. One forty-five.

"You ready, Caleb?" Garnet said.

"Huh? Oh, yeah."

Technically. The chairs for the four-seat lift detached onto a slower cable, so it wasn't an issue for him to be on foot. Other than his dignity, really, but he'd learned many a time throughout his schooling that if he kept his chin up and pretended to know what he was doing, people bought the lie.

He stepped forward. The chair hit the back of his knees, which locked. He stumbled. Nausea lurched in his throat. *Don't fall—*

Garnet threw her arm across his chest, forcing him to sit. "Do you need off?"

"Hell, no," he croaked. He braced his hands on his knees and swallowed as the chair switched to the faster cable. They accelerated up the hill, and Garnet brought the bar down. Caleb thought he caught an eye roll from one of the twenty-somethings they were sharing the chair with.

They could suck it. The restraint was the only thing stopping him from passing out right now.

"Caleb…" Her tone was concerned and curious and calm, but that was Garnet, so many things going on at once but somehow handling them in a way that projected utter competence, and holy crap, he always thought of himself as being competent, too, but it was damn impossible when his mind wouldn't stop racing and the wind was roaring, and— Oh, wait. That was blood rushing in his ears, not the wind.

Come on, lungs, work.

"Nice weather t-today." The words skipped between his teeth.

Garnet's eyes narrowed. "You don't have to push yourself like this."

A peal of panicked laughter escaped his tight chest. "What, you have a parachute?"

Gripping the metal bar, he took a deep breath. He was shoulder to shoulder with Garnet, something he'd have enjoyed were it not for the motion of the chair making him feel like he was going to topple forward any moment. To start rolling, churning in a wave of snow. A consuming roar. And then nothing.

No, not nothing. Then, yeah. But not now. *Focus on*

the sounds around you. Now, the cable hummed. A chilly gust whistled by. And Garnet was talking about something, was getting increasingly louder—

"Caleb." Her hand clasped his forearm with the same force as he gripped the safety bar. "Were you always afraid of heights?"

"No," he scoffed. Truthful, at least. "It's nothing that makes sense, Garnet."

Hell. So much for not being obvious about his anxiety. She'd noticed, the scoffing snowboarders sharing the chair had noticed… This was not going to work. No way could he show up for the party in the middle of a panic attack. And what were the chances she'd be interested in someone who struggled to sit on a chairlift?

He squeezed his eyes shut and groaned quietly.

"Post-traumatic stress doesn't have to make sense to be valid." With her poles stuck under her leg and her pack in her lap, she slid her gloved palm into his. His chest tightened, but with pleasure this time. It wasn't like he could feel much between layers of leather and polar fleece, but the sentiment grabbed him. She ran her thumb up and down his. The material of their gloves rasped. Was she going to try acupressure again, like she had the other afternoon?

Nope. Just handholding.

Huh.

He tightened his grip, glad she was on his left so that he didn't have to worry about his hand cramping up. He'd missed this connection, sharing a small, intimate gesture with another person.

Intimate? Seriously?

Yeah. Exactly that.

She wouldn't agree with him, though. She'd told him exploring the pull between them wasn't smart. Her willingness to get close to him began and ended with her obvious inclination to help people.

But even so, he couldn't forget the look in her eyes when he'd almost kissed her the other day. That spark of desire contradicted her words. Medicine had trained him to pursue clues and signs until he found a diagnosis. He wasn't going to get ahead of himself, but he wasn't going to write off that look, either. When something didn't line up, he couldn't not investigate it.

Garnet stood next to Caleb in line at the counter-service grill, watching him examine the menu board with serious brown eyes. No glasses today, and she kind of missed the stylishly geeky frames. His color was back to normal, and his hands were steady on his tray.

Good. She'd hated seeing his fear on the chairlift.

But one trip up the hill was not a problem solved.

Ten minutes on solid ground must have helped. They were in Creekview Lodge, the midstation building that housed a couple of eating establishments, bathrooms and first aid facilities. If he started to struggle again, she could find some privacy for him in the first aid room. But he seemed determined to push through.

"What can I get you?" he asked.

She jolted to attention and ordered her usual chicken quesadilla, then nudged him with her elbow. "Your money's no good here. I picked the place so I'll get the tab."

He stared at her, seeming to consider the offer for a few seconds before nodding. "I'll get the next one."

The next one. Warmth edged her ears. "Feeling optimistic?"

"Should I be?"

Her tray tipped a little, cutlery clinking against her

hot chocolate mug. She jerked to save it before the mug took a dive for the floor. It was like her brain was in one of those can't-run-fast-enough dreams, unable to accelerate to keep up with what was going on.

Holding his tray one-handed, he brushed his thumb across her cheek. His hungry gaze dipped from her lips down her body.

Oh, my. Her clothes were the epitome of shapeless—her patrolling jacket opened over ski pants and a quarter-zip athletic shirt—but the hunger in his eyes suggested he was more interested in tasting her mouth than the sandwich a cafeteria worker had just put up on the pass-through for him.

"I don't know," she blurted.

"I do," he said, putting their food on both their trays and guiding her toward the register. "But I'm not in a hurry."

A few minutes later they sat at a table for two on the edge of the bustle.

And given her brain was still stuttering like a car running out of gas, she couldn't get out the questions she really wanted to ask him. About his life prior to coming to Sutter Creek, prior to the avalanche. About what drove him to be in medicine. She'd have to rely on what was becoming the standard for them. "You still good for finding a DJ if I deal with decorations?"

Bemusement danced on his face. "You know, we don't always have to talk shop."

She shook her head slowly. She'd picked the lodge to eat so he couldn't avoid who she was, as much as to help him get over his fear of being up the mountain. "Talking shop *is* personal for me, Caleb. It's a big part of who I am."

His lips parted. One of his dark brows rose toward his hair, which was uncharacteristically tousled. A thrill teased her stomach. She flattened her palm to her solar plexus, telling herself to calm right down.

He chewed and swallowed, studying her. "You've had to fight for what you've gotten in life, haven't you?"

Her breath hitched. She had, but probably not in the way that he assumed. She'd fought with herself, fought to change her thought patterns so that she believed in where she was going and how she was getting there. That she could have the jobs she wanted and her parents would still love her, even if they made faces every time she mentioned things about work. That past put-downs and insults and mean-girl politics from high school and college needed to stay in the past, and not dating a guy who would keep her off the mountain, like she had in grad school. She had a solid group of friends who accepted her for who she was. *She* accepted herself for who she was.

"I—" Pressure built at the back of her throat, not wanting to release the words. *If he doesn't want to hear it, he's not worth it.* Inhaling deeply, she pushed forward. "Sort of. My parents made it very clear that quitting my master's program was a disappointment. But I was tired of doing something I hated for the sake of trying to fit in with them. Biochem wasn't my thing. *Academia* wasn't."

If he was in any way critical of that, he hid it behind a guarded expression. "One of my younger brothers went through that before finding his niche. Tough when you're a struggling musician with an academic-minded twin."

"And a surgeon for a brother."

He shrugged.

"So your parents weren't supportive?"

"They had high expectations *that* we succeed, but the field we succeeded in—up to us. I followed them into medicine, but that was my doing, not theirs. My brother Asher, though, he didn't always take them at their word, even though they were as supportive of him being in a band as they are now that he's a librarian."

She sighed and drew a circle in her sour cream with a quesadilla triangle. Despite a hard morning of skiing, she wasn't feeling hungry. "My parents gave lip service to my doing what makes me happy, but were disappointed when I didn't finish my degree."

"You didn't want to finish it before trying something else?"

She narrowed in on his face, but the question was based in inquisitiveness, not criticism. "I'd spent far too much of my life pretending to like things for the sake of fitting in—with my parents, boyfriends, friends, you name it. One more year of that…" Damn it. She didn't usually mind being open with people—had made it her MO, really—but her throat closed over before she could admit how stupid she'd been.

"Too high a price to pay?" he asked.

Correctly finishing her thought, too.

Wait. She wasn't here to talk about herself. If he didn't want to talk shop, as he put it, she could work on figuring out how to help him get comfortable on the mountain.

Or you could just enjoy being out for lunch with an intelligent, smoking-hot guy.

Sending him a half smile, she let herself appreciate the couple days' stubble highlighting the angle of his jaw. She could so happily stroke that roughness. Feel it against her lips…

His brown eyes glinted and his attention dropped to her mouth.

Oh. She was biting her lip again. Crap.

She relaxed her mouth, forcing herself to break the nervous gesture. "That's something for another day, I think."

"What's today for, then?"

She felt her teeth heading for her lip again, and she pushed against the inside of her bottom lip with her tongue instead. "You were the one who agreed to come. You tell me."

More tease than challenge colored her tone, and Caleb sent her a slow smile. "Just can't let go of the idea of mixing a little pleasure in among the business."

Her expression turned wary. "How about we finish with business first, and then consider pleasure?"

He sighed at her persistence and chewed a mouthful of his clubhouse sandwich. Not much ranked above locally raised bacon, even if it would make his cardiologist friends cringe. He'd made it up to midstation without totally losing it on the lift. He'd have to try once or twice more before the party, see if he could do it without panicking. And getting another sandwich like this would be a decent reward. "The food's fantastic here."

"Yup." She cocked a brow. "It's not my favorite Sutter Creek restaurant, though. That honor goes to the Aussie pie place. Have you tried it?"

Midchew, he shook his head.

"We should go there and shuffle through our co-workers' catering preferences over a pepper steak pie," she said.

"Or we could plan to meet at the Peak Lounge next." He was halfway up the mountain. Maybe next time he'd make it the whole way.

"That's what I like to hear."

He smiled.

Her gaze traveled to the digital clock affixed over the double-door entrance to the lounge. "And as much as I'd love to dally, I have to finish off my shift." Her smile faltered. "You going to be okay getting back down the hill?"

Embarrassment crept hot up his neck. "I was thinking of, uh, taking the gondola. I'll walk you out."

"Okay. I need to stop by the patrol shack on the way to my skis. Battery's getting low on my radio."

They cleaned up their trays and headed for the exit. A number of people waved at Garnet or tossed her a hello. A few were also decked out in patrol uniforms, others just skiing for fun. She graced each person with a wide smile.

He recognized her easy popularity. Envied it, even. He'd had that at the hospital back in Denver. Hadn't realized how much he'd enjoyed being the figurative big man on campus. Up until the point they'd switched to feeling sorry for him.

Flexing his perpetually aching hand, he rested it on her back, low under the pack she'd slung onto her shoulders. "Popular lady," he commented.

Her mouth turned up at the corner, and she put an arm around his waist, dishing out a friendly hip check. "Ever heard the one about flies and honey and vinegar?"

"Yeah, yeah," he murmured. "You fit in at Evolve, but you do up here, too. I've been wondering what you consider your job, and which one's the side gig."

"Both and neither." She didn't take her arm away. Walking down the busy hall with her tucked into his side was awesome. She smelled like handfuls of mint and rosemary, plus a hint of snow and clean sweat. That smell would be just right on his sheets.

His groin tightened at the thought.

"I don't see committing to either full-time at the moment," she continued as they walked in tandem down the front steps of the lodge toward a wooden outbuilding. Their boots crunched in the hard-packed snow. "I like both jobs, and I'm happy splitting my focus."

"Is it enough during the summer?"

"I do adventure guiding during the summer. Climbing and mountain biking, etcetera."

He swallowed against the sudden thickness in his throat. Unless he wanted to be a recluse, he'd have to get used to having friends who still enjoyed the risky hobbies that now scared the ever-loving crap out of him. But could he date a woman who was so different? Could they find enough in common? He pictured her hanging from a rock face, something he used to do for giggles, and a visceral palm slapped at his sternum. The warning pressure slowed his gait.

With Garnet's arm still around his waist, the change in speed caught her. She stumbled a little, and he gripped her hip to stop her from bailing. They were almost to the door of the little wooden shack, and she eyed him as she unlocked the code on the knob and led him inside.

The shack was cramped, though immaculately tidy. Someone had decorated for Christmas, with strands of colored lights crisscrossing on the ceiling and framing the small window. Dilapidated metallic garlands hung from the shelves that ran the wall on one side of the single room. Medical supplies and safety equipment neatly lined the open slats. The sled in the corner seemed to blink like a damned strobe light, egging on his memories of being strapped to a backboard minutes after being encased on all sides by cement-like snow.

The palm of panic on his chest dug in its fingers, taking hold of his lungs. He fought to keep his breath steady.

Garnet shifted to stand in front of him. After taking off her gloves, she stroked careful fingers along his forehead and down his cheeks, then cupped his jaw with one hand. "In and out. Easy, there."

He dropped his forehead to hers, the breath shuddering from his lungs. Echoes of rescuers' voices, working across the avalanche field, rang in his ears... *Sam! We found Sam...in shock... Losing him...* And the bone-deep relief Caleb had felt that he hadn't suffered the same fate. It had become as much a part of him as his scars and fears. And he'd hated it ever since.

Hated that part of himself.

"Is it the small space?"

"No." Taking off his own gloves, he found her hands and twined his fingers in hers. "The sled."

"I shouldn't have invited you in here."

"You couldn't have known." The gravel in his voice rattled his eardrums. "It's nothing *I* can predict, and it's my own damn brain."

She eased a little closer and turned her face, putting her cheek to his jacketed chest. She tightened her grip on his hands. "Snuck up on you?"

"Yeah." He rested his chin on the top of her head and took a deep breath. Some of the herbal scent he'd detected in the lodge was coming off her hair. Freaking perfection, that smell.

"If you ever need to talk, let me know. And my colleague works with biofeedback therapy—it's been shown to help with PTSD."

"I'll look into it." Tension leached from his muscles. Something about having Garnet plastered to his front. He could get used to holding this woman. And focusing on that rather than how all over the place his reactions were today... Yeah, Garnet won out, for sure. "Should have had lunch at the base lodge lounge."

"Probably."

He tilted her chin up with his finger. "That way we'd have a good chance of standing under that stupid mistletoe."

"Oh." She gasped. "I thought you meant..."

"I didn't."

"You meant—" Her lids lowered to half-mast and her lips parted.

"I meant I'd love the pretense so I could kiss you right now."

Letting go of his hands, she threaded her fingers behind his neck. "No pretense needed."

"Good to know." He lowered his head and tasted her mouth, finally getting to test the softness of her lips and how the angles of their bodies fit together. He walked her backward until they were pressed against the desk. Her fingers rasped against the jaw he'd been too lazy to shave, a purposeful, tactile exploration. He was all over that. Loving her hips under his palms, too. Three or four layers of ski gear made it hard to get the full effect of touching her, but he caught enough of the curve of her to enjoy it. And to want more.

To slowly unzip her jacket and sneak his fingers under her layers and test out the strength of the battered desk.

She teased his mouth with her tongue, sending a rush of need through his limbs to pool in his belly. Sweetness clung to her lips, the dregs of her hot chocolate.

"Mmm," she hummed, pulling her mouth away. Her cheeks were pink, and only a thin ring of gray rimmed her wide pupils. "You're good at that."

His chest rose and fell rapidly, having nothing to do with anxiety like before. "You too."

"I have to get to work, though."

A cold rivulet of dread trickled down his neck at the thought of her job, and he untangled from their embrace and linked his hands at his nape.

But even with the fear, something about her still pulled at him. And her kiss... *Whoa.*

He retreated a few steps. "Better not keep you."

Nodding, she unclipped her helmet off her pack and set to straightening her layers. "You busy tonight?"

"Wanting to fill up my dance card, Ms. James?"

She pulled on her gloves. "Trivia night at the Loose Moose. Want to come along?"

"Sutter Creek tradition, I'll bet?"

She smiled, her clear fondness for the town coming through. "Every second Monday."

"Wish I could. But I'm on call at the hospital tonight. My partners and I cover a few shifts a month each." His mother's reminders about tradition from their conversation the other day filtered to the surface. Maybe he could make her happy and make some connections to Sutter Creek at the same time, have a few people over to his place for once. "I'll make it up to you—come over for Hanukkah dinner this Friday."

Chapter Seven

Sorry, buddy. Garnet's just descending from the glacier and Lachlan's finishing up with the dog. Successful call, though. Found the missing skier. We'll be another hour or two.

Caleb read the text from Zach, and something undefinable twinged in his chest.

He glanced at the Frenched lamb racks in the roasting pan on the oven, their clean bones threaded together. Good thing he hadn't put the meat in yet.

This is what happened when two thirds of your dinner party volunteered for the local search and rescue branch. Hanukkah dinner got delayed when some idiot went out-of-bounds. The asshole was lucky he hadn't ended up four feet under a snowfield. Hell, two feet was enough when you had a shattered hand and broken leg. Caleb knew that all too well.

What he hadn't known was that Garnet was on Zach's team to begin with. He dabbed at his clammy forehead with the dishtowel he'd flung over his shoulder. *Make a decision, Matsuda.* Time to back slowly away from this woman, or to run toward her, eyes closed to all the parts of her that made him break into a cold sweat.

A few expletives ran through his head. Running toward her sounded way too risky, but small, measured steps could work. He couldn't keep letting one horrible day dictate the rest of his life. There was nothing wrong with having post-traumatic stress, but it didn't need to be the driver moving forward. He deserved to feel fulfilled. To adapt.

And really, wasn't that what dinner tonight was supposed to be? Adapting to having friends who spent a good deal of their time doing things Caleb could never see himself doing again?

An hour later, after he dealt with the purple potatoes and asparagus and cleaning all the prep dishes, Zach, Cadie and Marisol finally showed up, followed a few minutes later by Lachlan. No word from Garnet, though. Seemed kind of odd that she wouldn't text him once she was finished with her duties.

Cadie, standing next to him arranging an appetizer on a plate, caught him checking the clock on the microwave and grinned. "She'll be here."

"You sure?" His doubt spilled out before he could claw it back.

Grin softening to a knowing smile, Cadie squeezed his shoulder, then turned her head to shoot a dirty look at Zach. "Did you not pass on Garnet's message, babe?"

Zach took a pull from his beer bottle, and raised a puzzled eyebrow. "Yeah, I mentioned that she was stuck on the glacier like the rest of us."

"No, genius, that her cell died from being out of range."

"I was incident commander, doing eight things at once, *belleza*—I can't remember." Zach shrugged at Caleb. "Sorry if I forgot."

Relief lightened Caleb's chest.

Good grief. He had it way too bad for this woman. He waved off Zach's apology before sticking the lamb in the oven, his glasses fogging up from the heat. He curled his lip and blew air up at them until they cleared. "Was it a sticky rescue?"

Zach launched into a detailed story about Garnet up on the glacier that had sweat prickling at Caleb's hairline again, so when the doorbell rang, he was only too happy to answer it.

Her apologetic smile greeted him. In the gentle light of the strands of white bulbs he'd wrapped around the posts and rails on his front porch—he hadn't wanted to be the only person on his street without lights up—Garnet glowed. A hand-knit scarf circled her neck. Her knee-length black coat prevented him from telling what she had on underneath, but her shapely calves in bright teal tights made him smile. Ethereal, almost. She'd done something subtle to her eyes and a pink sheen highlighted her lips.

"Hey," he said, putting a hand on her shoulder and kissing her cheek. "You look fantastic."

"Thanks." She clutched a wine bag in one hand and a plastic-wrapped platter in another. He took the platter from her with a thank-you and rested it on the porch railing so that he could link his fingers through hers.

"Welcome," he said, all of a sudden wondering if his two-story house, modern and different from the others nearby, would stand up to the approval of a local. Not that he'd built it, but he'd still been in city mode when he'd bought the place.

She didn't even seem to be looking at it, though; she had her apologetic gaze fixed on his. "I'm so sorry I'm late. But there was no way I could come straight here without cleaning up, not after four hours of hiking and climbing and hauling a snarky twenty-year-old guy out of the wilderness on a sled."

Caleb exhaled before his lungs could seize up. "It's all good. Zach was keeping me updated."

"Yeah, Zach. Not me. And I couldn't get my cell to work when I got home, either. I think the battery's shot." Her gaze flitted from the open neckline of his dress shirt to his waist and up to his face. A silver spark of desire lit her eyes. She leaned in to return the cheek kiss. Her breath warmed his night-air-chilled ear. "You look fantastic, too. Your glasses...they make you look really... I mean, they suit you."

"I'll wear them more often, then." He grinned. She was hatless, and a mass of loose-but-tamed curls spilled over her shoulders. He inhaled as subtly as he could, enjoying the scent of mint and woman.

She rested her cheek to his chest for a second and went to give him a hug, but stopped, and stepped back, holding out her still-full right hand. Her face screwed up with uncertainty. "I brought wine, but I understand if you can't accept a gift. I'll leave it in my car and give it to you another time... I mean, I looked up Jewish holidays online, and I read not to bring host gifts after sundown for Shabbat, but I wasn't sure the same rules applied to Hanukkah and—"

He stroked her cheek, letting his thumb linger near the corner of her mouth. "You read up on Hanukkah?"

She nodded.

"Dreidels and gelt?"

"That was mentioned."

Damn, he needed to taste her mouth. Tilting his head, he dropped a soft kiss to her lips, savoring the hint of sweetness in her gloss. She tasted better than anything he had roasting in the kitchen. A frigid blast of wind made goose bumps rise on his forearms, but he didn't much care about being out in the cold in only his shirtsleeves, not when it meant he got a private space of time with Garnet. He brushed a kiss at the base of her ear. Reveled in her shiver against his mouth. "What did Google say about lamb and potatoes?"

"Didn't come across that." Her hand rested on the placket of buttons on his shirt. He slid a hand along her waist, disguised as it was by the belt on her coat. Her fingers tensed against his chest and her lips parted.

"Well, that's what I'm making. And I'm not observant, Shabbat or otherwise. I'm hoping you have a bottle of red wine hidden in that bag, because nothing complements a good cut of lamb like something with a bit of body or spice to it."

A wide smile crossed her face. "Body or spice? There's a cheesy, suggestive comment somewhere in that statement."

He took the wine bag by the handles and used the transfer as an excuse to catch her fingers and brush a kiss across her knuckles. "My mother smacked all the cheesy suggestion out of me while I was still impressionable."

"There's room in feminism for a little innuendo now and again," she murmured, stealing another quick kiss.

Tracing his thumb along her plush lower lip, he sent her a rueful look. "If we stay out here much longer, everyone's going to know what we've been up to."

She blinked, and the corners of her mouth turned down. "I wasn't particularly worried about that, but if you are…"

He hated putting that look on her face, the trace of sadness that stole from what he'd thought was an endless reserve of joy. Ignoring the cold threatening to form ice crystals in his hair, he put the wine next to the plate she'd brought and tugged on her waist, bringing her flush with his body. "Then again, I doubt anyone's going to care."

Their lips touched. A rush of need tumbled through him, racing along his skin. His pants weren't going to be flat-fronted anymore, not at this rate. The mint on her lips flooded his tongue. He wanted to dig his hands into her hair, but figured she wanted the strands to be purpose-fully teased, not actually messy. He kept his hand at her waist and settled the other on her neck, tilting her back a little and slowing the kiss. The whimper of complaint against his mouth, her fingers tensing on his back urging him to speed up again, had him groaning.

A too-fast warning bell clanged in his brain. The world blurred, like he was on the slope in flat light without the right color of goggles. Backing off, he glanced to the side, pretended to adjust one of the strands of clear lights.

They'd probably overstayed their welcome on the porch.

Their friends getting the wrong idea was one thing. But would he be able to give this woman what she deserved? Was he being selfish by pursuing even casual dating? He didn't know if he could handle her working for SAR. He respected it, absolutely. But it scared the crap out of him.

As did the way kissing her felt like way more than just a kiss.

Because the heat in her expression suggested things could go from casual to something more damn quick.

"Caleb… That keeps getting…" She brought her fingers to her lips and an audible exhalation shuddered from her lungs.

"Yeah." He swallowed. "Good thing, or bad thing?"

Before she could answer, Zach stuck his head out the door. His gaze flicked between Garnet's hand-covered mouth and Caleb's face, and he shook his head. "The timer dinged on your quiche things."

"Take them out, then," Caleb grumbled. He cupped Garnet's elbow and nudged her toward the door. "Come in and warm up."

Though if she was anything like him, her body would be smoking from that kiss for days.

Garnet spent most of dinner feeling a little distant from the rest of the group. Stunned, probably, were she being honest with herself. It wasn't a matter of the conversation being stilted. Caleb and Lachlan had spent a good part of dinner—the small part when Lachlan wasn't watching Marisol like he wanted to drag her to one of Caleb's guest bedrooms and test out the springiness of the mattress, that is—talking about veterinary medicine. Caleb had apparently picked up a fair amount of knowledge from one of his younger brothers, who was a vet in upstate New York. And Zach and Cadie had been their usual social selves. Only Marisol had been quiet, admitting she was sad about her time with her brother and his family coming to an end.

Garnet wasn't sure how she wanted her own night to end. She could go for a little more distraction of the kissing variety. Their porch kiss had stolen her ability to think for a good hour. Her leg muscles were reminding her she'd had a long day—an early morning patrol shift on avalanche control, and the rescue in the afternoon. But her lips were still in good shape.

Lachlan left first after dinner, and Garnet was up to her wrists in sudsy water, working on a stubborn crusty bit on the roasting pan, when Zach plucked a tea towel off the handle of the oven. "I can dry."

"Caleb said to let 'em air dry."

"I'll just grab our plate, then." He wiggled a white serving plate out of the half-full sink of clean dishes and polished off the drips. "We're going to take off. I'm covering a shift in the morning, and Cadie's driving Marisol to the airport. Need a ride home?"

"I drove here," Garnet said.

"I know."

"I've only had a glass of wine. I'm fine."

Zach tightened his lips. "It's not that. I wasn't sure…"

She bristled at his hesitance. "Am I okay to be here alone, you mean."

He shrugged.

"Why wouldn't I be?"

"Caleb's a great guy." He sighed, glancing over his shoulder in what looked like a check to make sure the other three remaining members of the party were out of earshot across the open space. "But he's still dealing with the aftermath of the avalanche. And dating someone who's processing trauma can get complicated. Finding a place of balance with Cadie—for both my reasons and hers—was one of the hardest things I've ever had to do. And no offense, but you don't seem to be much for sticking in relationships."

She narrowed her eyes. "No offense? How could I take that any other way?" The knee-jerk defensiveness speeding up her heart rate rang clear in her tone.

Zach hadn't known her in high school, didn't know about the *flaky* label she'd earned due to her chameleon changes of heart. She'd earned that label. But Zach's wariness chafed at five years spent proving she was no longer the girl with quicksilver habits.

He dropped his head and shook it. "I just don't want either of you to get hurt."

Like she wasn't aware of that? *Grrr.* "No need to go all condescending boss on me."

He winced. "Sorry. Look, I love the guy like a brother, and you're one of my favorite people, no exaggeration, but I'm not sure you fit together."

"All right, Fairy Godmother. I'll take that under advisement."

He sent a beleaguered glance at the angled ceiling.

"I'll see you at work, Zach," she said, pointedly dismissing him.

He squeezed her shoulder and opened his mouth, but paused, long enough that she figured his "See ya" didn't encompass all his thoughts.

His footsteps faded across the room, followed by the goodbyes being shouted from the front hall. She called out a farewell and tried to get excited about being alone in the house with Caleb, but couldn't shake Zach's criticism. *I'm not sure you fit together.*

Son of a... She balled the dishcloth and threw it into the sink. Water splashed against the stainless steel sides.

Socked footsteps sounded on the hardwood, a different gait than Zach's.

Two strong arms bracketed her, hands planting on the edge of the sink. A thrill ran up her spine. Having Caleb's hard body at her back, him touching her for the first time since they came in off the front porch, made her skin tingle. *Good job picking the thin sweater dress instead of something bulkier.* With only a layer of knit and his dress shirt between them, the relief of his chest muscles was obvious against her shoulders.

"You're working too hard," he said, nuzzling her ear. The arm of his glasses creaked, sandwiched between their faces.

She stayed focused on the dishes. The warmth of him and his cologne curling into her senses and the chill-out music on the built-in speakers made it difficult. "I can't relax until the kitchen is clean."

He nipped her earlobe. "Sure about that?"

Knees jellying, she closed her eyes and rested her head

against his shoulder while he kissed a path along the boat-neck opening of her dress. "I grew up with parents who insisted on a full breakfast and doing the dishes before we opened presents on Christmas morning. I can withstand anything."

Sliding his hands from the counter to her hips, he tugged her flush against his front—oh, Lordy, his chest wasn't the only hard thing about him. His tongue traced a hot path along her collarbone. Stubble tickled her shoulder. Gentle, sensuous movements that sparked along her skin and stoked the embers at her core into flame.

"Anything?" he asked.

She'd thought so. But his hand, palm lying flat on its journey up her belly to her ribcage, was making a fool of her assertions.

"Caleb," she said on a breath. It came out a whimper instead of her intended warning.

"I knew this would be more fun without ski clothes on."

"This would be more fun without any clothes on," she blurted. Heat rushed into her cheeks.

"Good thing everyone else left." He chuckled against her ear. "You in a rush?"

As a matter of fact, yes. Her skin clamored for his touch. It had been too long since she'd had a guy's hands on her.

She stripped off the dish gloves and spun in his embrace, leaning back against the counter and holding him to her like he'd done. She rose on her toes, trying to better nestle her front against his hips—

Oh, fine. She was trying to grind against him.

Classy, James. Super classy.

His fingers dug into her hips and his eyes shuttered halfway. "Garnet..."

So maybe he didn't mind so much.

"What—" Settling a hand at her waist, he cupped the back of her head with the other. He cuddled her close and buried his face in her hair. "What are we doing here, Sharky?"

Damn. What *were* they doing?

"Aside from trying to climb each other like trees?" she croaked.

His laugh vibrated through her body. "Yeah."

"I—I'm honestly not sure."

"Nor I." His breath tickled her ear, and her uncertainty made her knees shake. His arms tightened around her, and she let him take her weight.

"I think we need to talk," she said.

"Uh-oh."

"No, no. Not in a bad way. But if we're going to go forward, it should be with intent. Reasoned intent, not just the get-in-your-pants kind."

He exhaled noisily and released her, rocking back on his heels. "Okay. More wine, then?"

"Definitely."

They settled on the gray tweed sectional in his living room. He angled slightly toward her, stretching an arm along the low back of the couch. The stem of a glass of Australian Syrah balanced between two of his fingers.

Curling next to him, she drew up her knees and clenched her own wineglass in both hands.

"Before we get into the nitty gritty, I want you to know—" The corner of his mouth tugged up. "You make me smile. I've missed smiling."

Her heart caught in her chest. Her wineglass slipped in her grip.

He rescued it before she managed to slop any of the

deep red liquid onto the wide cushions. "Easy there, but-terfingers."

"Sorry, but Caleb—that's a hell of a starting point." She resettled her hand around the bulb of the glass and took a long drink.

He brushed a finger down her cheek. "You thinking of driving home tonight? Or no?"

"I probably shouldn't stay. Not tonight."

He nodded slowly, flattening his lips before he adopted a placid expression. "Of course."

"I don't have to rush home, though. And this is pretty delicious wine. I could take a taxi."

Genuine pleasure deepened the grooves at the corners of his eyes. Gah, why did men in their thirties have to look so good with crow's feet? Freaking unfair. At least, she thought he was in his thirties. Possible he was older than he looked, though, given how far he'd climbed the surgery ladder in Colorado.

She didn't care much about age, but she was curious. "How old are you?"

"Thirty-eight."

She caught her smile before it faltered. She might not be fazed by a ten-year age difference, but was he? "You've got a decade on me."

"Mostly spent slogging in the OR." The open neck of her sweater had gaped to the side, and he traced a lazy circle with the back of a finger.

A spritz of shivers danced along her flesh. "All work and no play?"

He shook his head. "If I wasn't in the hospital, I was out in the backcountry. And I had a long-term girlfriend."

"Both things that changed." *Damn it. Filter, Garnet, filter.*

If her nosiness bothered him, it didn't show. His gaze

stayed on her, steady and deep brown. "The avalanche taught me to slow down. And my girlfriend at the time didn't much like that. We didn't have enough in common anymore."

"Do we have the same problem?"

He stared into his wineglass. "Probably."

Fear bolted from her gut to her throat. She chewed on the inside of her lip. "Okay, then. Maybe I should head home, after all."

His chin jerked up and he pinned her with a worried expression. "No. Just because we don't have everything in common doesn't invalidate what we do have."

"Which is…"

"A draw, Garnet. That indefinable thing that makes you want more of a person. You're a package of mysteries, and something's pulling me to discover what's hidden underneath your well of energy and beautiful smile."

She coughed out the lump of emotion gathering in her throat. "Aren't you good with words."

"And other things." The promise in his unabashed smile made her mouth go a little dry.

She sensed that indefinable thing, too. Didn't come around often, and wasn't something to take for granted and ignore. And testing herself, seeing if she could be with someone and not lose herself in the process… She might be ready for that.

Chapter Eight

Caleb appreciated Garnet's hesitance. He also found the contemplative crinkle between her auburn brows damn adorable. He took a sip of wine and put his glass on the coffee table, then stroked a palm along her cheek. His hand was throbbing after all the chopping he'd done for dinner, and he'd probably be better off medicating with ibuprofen than wine.

Even when his mind tried to avoid his past and how it clashed with Garnet's present and future, his body wouldn't let him forget.

"I didn't know you volunteered for SAR before I got Zach's text today," he admitted.

"Had I not mentioned it?"

He shook his head.

She sighed. "One more deal breaker?"

"Depends on whether you need me to be in the thick of the SAR scene. I volunteered back in Colorado, but even if I wanted to, with my hand I wouldn't be able to recertify for backcountry rescue. Nor do I see adding wilderness adventures back into my free time."

"Why'd you move here, then?"

Her question was soft, not critical. He shrugged. "Some ill-thought-out attempt at exposure therapy. And probably a dose of pride, too."

She studied him, eyes serious. "I don't want to force

you to be something you're not any more than I don't want to lose who I am."

"I thought I'd be a green circle kind of guy from now on," he admitted, trying to throw in a reference to the designation of the easiest ski run system to lighten the mood.

"I'll bet you did." Compassion softened her expression. "Green circles aren't enough for me, Caleb. I'm not an easy-run kind of girl."

"Nor should you be," he said, trying to echo both her understanding tone and her words. He picked up her wineglass-free hand and clasped it between both of his.

She squeezed his fingers. "Think I could convince you to up your game a little? Give a blue square a try?"

Medium difficulty? He took a slow breath. "Which would look like what?"

"A literal blue square run, Caleb. I don't need to share every last interest with you. You don't need to recert for SAR, or want to go into the backcountry, but I'd really like to be able to take some turns with you now and again. On the boring old blue groomers. Nary an unstable slope in sight."

He hadn't thought he'd ever consider skiing again. But then, he hadn't thought he'd get on a chairlift, either... A lump formed at the back of his throat, turning his "maybe" into a croak.

Her fingers tightened around his again. "Friends is okay, too."

Dregs of arousal still lingered from having her body pressed to his, disagreeing with her. "No, Garnet. I'm not sure it is."

The rest of her wine disappeared in one gulp. She set her empty glass next to his on the table. Scooted closer, draping one long leg over his thigh. "You have a point."

"I know." Gripping her hips, he tugged until she straddled his lap. Her dress shifted up, exposing taut thighs in those bright tights. And the fit of her against his hardness...

Oh. Damn.

Yeah.

Heat pooled behind the fly of his pants. He dropped his head to the back of the couch and groaned.

Shifting in his lap, settling her soft center over him, she whimpered. Her lashes formed dark crescents above freckled cheeks.

He stroked the outsides of her thighs. Her skin would be smooth and pale, or maybe freckled like her face in places, and damn, he wanted to explore every inch to find out.

"I like having you at my mercy," she murmured, walking her fingers up his chest and nipping at the skin of his neck with her pretty lips and the smallest scrape of teeth. She slid his glasses off and laid them on the side table. The world beyond her blurred without the corrective lenses.

Hell, with her so close, the world beyond didn't exist.

She speared her hands into the sides of his hair and brought her mouth to his.

A hint of warning broke through the need fogging his brain. He'd meant his *maybe*. Wasn't ready to say *yes* yet. And until he was, he needed not to get in over his head.

No reason he couldn't make her feel good, though.

Shifting until he sprawled on his side—good move, buying the couch with the wide cushions—he tugged her against him and kissed her. Her touch felt damn right, gripping his shirt hard enough to pop a button. She threw a leg over his hips, circling against his groin again. Had he ever lost himself in a woman like he was in Garnet?

They'd fit together perfectly if they were naked.

Not wanting to give any less pleasure than she was to

him, he cupped her ass and stroked his other hand up her ribs. Traced the curve of her breast with a thumb, eliciting a breathy sigh.

When they finally came up for air, her hands were tangled in his hair and her lips were swollen. He pressed a gentle kiss to the glossy pink flesh.

Her throat bobbed and her chest rose and fell like the rough chop of a stormy ocean. Sprawled half on him, half on the couch, she tucked her head under his chin. His heart rate was flying, like it used to do when he'd bomb his way through first-tracks powder.

Hers was, too. The vibration thrummed against his chest. "So how about you tell me what to do for this night to end how you want it to end?"

"Good question." She yawned wide, and her jaw clunked.

Classic sound of someone who ground their teeth in their sleep, and his professional curiosity got the best of him. "You grind your teeth, Sharky?"

"Now and again."

"Thought you'd be stress-free."

"No one's stress-free, Caleb." She shifted up a little, covering more of his front until he was flat on his back and she was doing her best blanket impression. "I'll move in a second, promise. This is really nice, though. Jesus, you smell good."

He grinned into her hair. The desperation of their kissing was fading. Oh, he could find it again. Minute their lips touched, guaranteed. But this, holding her, feeling her body grow pliant—was just as enjoyable as frantic need.

She had to be exhausted after a long rescue. Scrubbing his knuckles lightly on her back, he soaked in the pleasure of having a woman draped across his body.

"You really should come skiing with me," she said, words slurring with sleep. "I'll keep you safe."

An impossible promise to keep. But something about her tired determination convinced him she'd do her damnedest to try.

The moon cast a glaring white stripe across the living room when Garnet woke. She'd slid off Caleb at some point, but the couch cushion was deep enough to hold them both. Wrapped tight in each other, they almost had room to spare.

The temperature of the room had fallen, and her cheeks were a little chilled. The rest of her was toasty, though. Caleb had pulled a luscious knit throw off the back of the couch and covered them with it. Between that and the heat of him at her back, she couldn't remember the last time she'd been this cozy. She was using his arm as a pillow, but the crick in her neck was a worthy price to pay for getting to be the little spoon to his big one.

Don't get too comfortable. Literally, or figuratively.

She winced at the inner warning. Was she actually going to consider breaking her dating moratorium for him? A "maybe" to her ski invitation was a step for him— she saw that. She wasn't going to hold the fact he was still healing against him.

But what if, as he healed, he decided it wasn't healthy to be with someone who loved things so closely tied to his trauma? If he asked her to cut back on something she loved because it was a trigger for him? Her ex had pretended to be supportive at the beginning. Maybe Caleb—

No. She needed to stop with the hypotheticals. They were just having a good time with each other. Nothing serious. For now, she'd just be aware of not repeating past mistakes. She wouldn't put her interests aside to the point of sacrificing her self-worth again.

And speaking of her interests, she needed to get home. Which sadly required moving.

Caleb still lay on his back. She didn't want to extract herself from his embrace, not really. Part of her wanted to stay close like this for a long, long time.

But she wasn't ready to wake up in the actual morning with him and navigate the uncomfortable "do we have breakfast—do we not—should I cook for you" territory. If she left now, she could swing another sleep cycle or two before her patrolling shift.

Mustering the will to peel out of his muscular arms, she sat.

He grumbled, nothing audible in words.

"Caleb?" Tracing a hand down his stubbly cheek, she kissed his forehead. "You awake?"

"Wh' time is it?"

She glanced at the clock on the cable box. "Three."

A big hand landed on her shoulder and tugged.

"No. I gotta go."

He cracked a lid to half open. "You sure, Jewel?"

She snorted at the completely unoriginal rendering of her name. "I'll give you a pass on that one given you're half-asleep."

"I'll figure something out that's more romantic than an ocean predator." Frowning, he unfolded himself and sat next to her, covering her hand where it rested on the couch. "You don't want to stick around? I make a mean omelet."

A frisson of awareness ran up her spine. No matter how much she wanted to create healthy boundaries, she also really, really liked the idea of eventually having breakfast with this guy. On a day where they'd preplanned and whatnot, avoiding the awkward. "Not today. Another time."

"Another time…" His mouth tilted. "You working Sunday?"

She leaned into his side and savored the warmth and faded cologne at his neck. "Nope."

"Excellent," he murmured into her hair. His voice was thick, edging on strained. "How about you take me skiing, then?"

The following afternoon, Garnet gripped one of the coatrack hooks in the Evolve staff room with one hand and her phone in the other, cursing the lack of a blinking text notification light.

Maybe confirming ski-date details via text wasn't the best way to go. She'd sent the message on her lunch break and figured she'd get a reply by the end of her shift, but nope.

After tossing the device in the front flap of her backpack, she zipped her jacket. She'd walked to work in the sunshine this morning but a bank of clouds had rolled in over the course of the day, and with it, a hell of a wind. The five blocks to her apartment was going to feel like fifty if she didn't bundle up.

Footsteps tapped softly on the carpet.

"Sharky." Two hands landed on her hips, making her jump. A low, sexy voice growled, "I like it better when you're taking layers off."

"Caleb!"

"Sorry to startle you. Lauren told me to come find you here."

She spun, wedging herself between the wall of jackets and his hard body in the process. He wore dark jeans and a navy wool coat, and those thick-rimmed glasses that tempted her to suggest they play professor-student.

His palms teased under her jacket. "You sure you want to zip this up?"

"Well, I'm definitely not going to strip down in the staff room!" she whisper-shouted.

"A shame."

Her mouth went dry. "Is it?"

"I think so."

"You didn't seem in a hurry to get back to me about skiing." She cringed and looked away when humor lit his dark eyes.

He ran the pad of his thumb just under her lower lip. "Why do you think I'm here?"

Fingers flexing into the wool at his shoulders, she swallowed. "You all of a sudden got hit by the need to decide on the catering menu?"

"I didn't want to wait until tomorrow to see you." Closing his eyes for a second, he stepped back. "Sorry. Someone could walk in. Inappropriate."

"Exactly." Having a little space between them allowed her to breathe better. She wrapped her scarf around her neck.

He rubbed his cheek with a flat hand. "When do we have to get the catering order in by?"

"Tuesday."

"I think everyone's responded to the survey, so I'll take a look at the results tonight and send the email off with our final numbers," he offered.

Skiing and catering? You're two for two in things she wanted from him. Maybe try for a third. Staff room be damned.

Closing the space between them, she sneaked her fingers under the lapel of his coat. She tilted her lips to his, silently asking for a kiss.

He settled his mouth over hers. More than his kiss

drew her in. It was his hand at her nape and the other at her waist, supporting her as she melted against him. It was the way he was the right height for her arms to loop easily around his neck. The thick, silky hair and strong shoulders and delicious, masculine cologne...

The door swung open, and Lauren walked in, scanning something in her massive wedding binder. She looked up, a crinkle between her blond brows. She laid the binder on one of the lunch tables and grinned widely. "Could you two be any cuter?"

Garnet sprang away from Caleb. Crap. "Oh, we're not—" She cut off the denial. She didn't know what they were, but it wasn't nothing.

She glanced at Caleb, who lifted an utterly unhelpful shoulder. His eyes were a bit glazed.

"Looked like a whole lot of *are too* to me." Lauren's nose scrunched and she pressed her fingers against her ribs.

"It shouldn't be an ethical issue for us to date," Garnet said in a rush. "He's not a client, and you know Sutter Creek—it's too small to avoid dating people you have professional connections with."

Face softening, Lauren shook her head. "It's the opposite of my business, Garnet."

"You made a face."

"Yeah, Mia Hamm here kicked me in the diaphragm."

"You know you're having a girl?"

Lauren grinned. "Nope. We're going to be surprised."

"Nice." There was a sweetness to that that Garnet appreciated. She'd probably want to be surprised, too.

Caleb linked fingers with Garnet and tugged her to his side. He dipped his head to her ear. "Dinner?"

"Sure."

"Couldn't. Be. Any. Cuter," Lauren emphasized, drawing an air frame around them with her pointer fingers.

"You're just seeing romance everywhere because you're getting married in three weeks," Garnet complained.

"That may be true." Lauren's eyes lit. "Caleb, you should come! Be Garnet's plus-one."

He blinked. "To what?"

"The wedding! New Year's Eve." Her face fell. "You're probably busy. I'm insulting you with the late invite."

He shook his head ruefully. "I'm free."

"Great, then." Lauren moved to her binder and scribbled something on a page with a pen she pulled out of a plastic slot in the cover.

Garnet stood on her toes to whisper, "You don't have to be my date."

Frustration marred his brow. He pressed a kiss to her cheek. "Stop. I want to do this." The words were barely audible. "I—I've wanted to feel like part of the crowd since I moved here."

Oh... She bit her lip and nodded.

"And I want to go with you," he said, no longer whispering.

Her cheeks heated.

"Tell you what—meet me in the foyer in five, okay?" he said.

She furrowed her brow in question.

His mouth twitched, and he dropped a kiss to her forehead. "I'm going to see about making an appointment. And then we can go have some of that pepper steak pie you're always raving about."

"Always?" she protested, but he was already out the door.

Lauren grimaced and made an "oops" face. "I pushed too hard, didn't I?"

"Don't worry about it. We're going skiing tomorrow— I'll make sure he really wants to attend."

Curiosity lit Lauren's eyes a clear green. "Sounds like you know him more than you're letting on."

Did she really know him? Not enough to quell her nerves. "We're not serious. We've barely been on a date."

"Not what I heard."

Their involvement had made the gossip rounds? Great. "I'm not counting coffee—that was about work. And playing pool was a group thing, as was dinner last night—"

"Cadie said you stayed late." Lauren's curious expression had morphed into downright nosiness. "Did you stay over?"

Garnet ignored the statement and went back to sorting the referral forms.

"Ha, you so did!"

"Not exactly."

You. So. Did, Lauren mouthed.

"I slept in my own bed." *And on him.* "I barely convinced him to go skiing. I'm pretty surprised he agreed to the wedding." Or at least, she'd stick to that story. She got the sense Caleb didn't want the whole world knowing his admission. When he'd confessed he wanted to fit in—holy moly, she wanted to help him do that. "Weddings are couple stuff."

"And you're a couple." By her singsong tone, Lauren was enjoying this way too much. "Also, I thought he didn't ski."

Agreeing to come with her counted as a big step for him. Garnet wasn't quite sure what had convinced him, but she'd take it as a good sign. Hope filled her previously shaky stomach, making her feel buoyant. Maybe his willingness to try skiing canceled out his nerves around her SAR volunteering…

Don't make excuses for him. Do not *get back into that habit.*

She shook her head. "We're not a couple yet."

Lauren smiled, appearing unconvinced. "I didn't think Tavish and I were a couple, and then he found me hiding on a picnic table at my brother's wedding, and let's just say I didn't much pay attention to the fireworks."

Garnet glared playfully. "Weren't you *already* pregnant by Andrew's wedding?"

"Well, yeah, but—" An impish shoulder lift hammered home how little Lauren cared about Garnet's protests.

Garnet rolled her eyes, not bothering to point out how their situations were completely different. If the bride-to-be wanted to believe that magic would happen at her wedding, Garnet wasn't going to disabuse her of the notion. She'd just reinforce to Caleb that it didn't mean they were serious.

She pulled on her knitted hat and put on her backpack. "I think my five minutes are up. And pie waits for no one."

Lauren's goodbye faded in her ears as she left the room and sped toward the entrance, curiosity driving her steps.

Caleb waited by the fireplace, hands jammed in his pockets.

She slowed. That wasn't the posture of a man looking forward to dinner and skiing and a wedding... Crap. Had his confident acceptance in the staff room been an act?

Mimicking his hands-in-pockets stance, she halted a foot to his right. "Hey."

He wrapped his arm around her shoulders and pulled her against him. "Fire's nice. And the mosaic is stunning."

"Weighs a ton," she said, staring at the locally crafted wood piece that had taken a team to maneuver onto the wall. "What's with the appointment?"

"I'm going to give biofeedback a try," he said. "I meant what I said—I want to feel like a part of this town, and to do that, I need to get right with the mountain. Exposure therapy's one thing—we'll see how skiing goes—but I need to give something else a shot, work on controlling my stress responses."

"I've heard good things." She bumped him with her hip. "You know what else is known to work?"

"What?"

"Pie."

He chuckled. "So you keep saying."

"Consider it a part of your fitting-in-to-Sutter-Creek mission."

Maybe that's why he's so interested in you. He's using you. Wow. That was a new one from the mental peanut gallery. She told the doubt to screw off as they linked hands and headed for the restaurant.

The cozy bistro should have been romantic as anything. And he oohed and aahed in all the right ways as they licked peppery gravy off forks and ate every last bite of flaky crust. She wanted to take his behavior at face value. But it was way too easy to slide back into thought patterns established by years of poor self-confidence. Even a table for two and to-die-for pastry couldn't erase the lingering suspicion that she was a means to an end for Caleb.

Chapter Nine

Caleb hefted his rented skis over his shoulder and loped toward the gondola as well as he could while wearing clunky ski boots. Why had he sold his top-of-the-line, comfortable equipment again?

You swore you were going to stay off the slopes for the rest of your life.

Right. That.

Well, one day of appeasing Garnet did not a rejuvenated ski career make. He'd try it for today. Get good enough with being on the mountain so that he could attend the party without having a flashback and sweating through his suit.

Easy runs only.

No promises beyond that.

There were two base-to-midstation lifts up the mountain: the quad near the base lodge and the gondola just off the town square. Garnet had asked him to meet at the gondola. A strategy to get him up the hill without having to put on skis right away? If so, kudos to her. Walking toward the black cubes wasn't jacking his pulse nearly as much as had the previous anticipation of going up the chairlift with her. Sure, he still sounded like an asthma patient. But that was an improvement on cardiac arrest victim, so he'd roll with it.

When they'd woken up on his couch in the nebulous hours between Friday night and Saturday morning, he hadn't wanted to let her go. Had known he needed to do something to guarantee seeing her again. So he'd decided to compromise. No way could he handle major vertical, but it would be fun to see her carving turns, even if it would be a hell of a lot easier than she could handle.

Than you can handle, too.

Ignoring the voice inside before it could convince him to push his limits, he scanned the crowd at the base of the lift for wild red hair and a pair of gray eyes with the power to wreck him.

And she just might.

The temptation to let himself fall tugged at his core. But he needed to be careful. She'd pulled back from him when they'd shared dinner last night, and he needed to figure out why before he let himself get any deeper.

He spotted her smile first. A sunlit spread of pretty lips and white teeth that made his pulse pick up for reasons entirely unrelated to anxiety. Her bright purple jacket stood out in the Sunday morning crowds. She waved madly to get his attention. The thick braid lying over one of her shoulders shifted.

Boots clunking on the bare cement, he breathed deeply to make sure his breakfast stayed in his stomach where it belonged, halting a few feet in front of her.

He tugged on her braid with a gloved hand. "I've gotten used to seeing your hair down."

The playful brightness she'd exuded after his Hanukkah dinner was still dimmed. "Maybe later."

"I hope you change that to a promise."

"Oh, yeah?" She sounded downright doubtful.

"Very much."

Their hands were too full of ski equipment to hug, but she scooted closer and awkwardly went up on the stiff toes of her boots to peck his lips.

"Weak, James."

She switched her poles to the hand already holding her skis and used her now-free hand to pull his face lower. "So sorry."

He groaned at the hint of cocoa on her lips, the intoxicating mix of firm and soft. Heaven. Seriously. "Keep doing that all day and I won't even notice you're dragging me up a mountain."

"Noted."

She kept distracting him as they waited in the gondola line, then slotted their equipment into the door holders and climbed on board. Every time he started to tense up, she seemed to know. Checked him in small ways— a hand to the chest, a quick kiss, a long one if he needed it—enough that in no time, they stood overlooking a run that he would have been able to ski with his eyes closed before the avalanche.

Now, after disembarking and snapping into his skis, he was sweating just taking in the blue square on the sign. Why couldn't it be overcast today? The too-bright sun seared his retinas. White dominated his vision.

Better than blue.

It had been blue inside the snow. And it had weighed on his chest just like his muscles were now. His throat tightened.

It's physiological. You can breathe. Get over it.

He stared out at the view of the town. The part of his brain that no longer acted logically sucked ass.

"Beautiful up here," he croaked.

Her brow furrowed and she sidestepped in front of him and glided forward, framing his skis with hers. "Looks like I need to kiss you again."

"I'm fine."

"You don't want to kiss me?" Her voice teased, but the wideness of her eyes contradicted her tone.

Crap. Did he look like he was in such bad shape? "I always want to kiss you. Why the heck do you think I'm here?"

Doubt crossed her face, then disappeared. Poles dangling from her wrists, she reached up to stroke his cheeks. "Because you're brave. And deep down, you know we're going to have fun today."

His heart pounded against ribs that were solidifying into steel bands.

"Tell me five things you can see, Caleb."

"Uh, why?" The words pushed against his tongue as he forced them out.

"Humor me."

Might as well play along. He sure wasn't ready to ski down the hill. "Trees. Snow. Sky's incredible." His mouth resisted turning up at the corners. "So are you. Love your freckles."

Her hands shifted from his face to his waist. "And four things you can feel?"

Ah, so that's where she was going with this. An anchoring technique. His therapist had taught him to make lists of things, but he'd try something new if it meant fending off a panic attack. Spots formed on the edges of his vision, and he tried to take in more air.

"Four things you feel," she repeated.

"My boots—too tight. Tag's itching my neck." He swallowed. "Gloves are fleecy inside. And your hands." She drew them away, and he shook his head. "No. Keep them there."

"Three things you hear," she said.

"My heartbeat."

"Fast?"

"Getting slower." And the inflexible band around his chest was loosening, too. Nothing was going to go wrong on a freaking blue run. He knew that. But her calming technique was working. Better finish. "And I hear skis cutting into snow. And the hum of the gondola."

"Good."

"Two things I can smell?" he said.

"You know it."

He sucked in a deep breath, managed to fill his lungs most of the way. "Winter. And rosemary." Her words from the other night popped into his head, and he echoed them back to her. "Jesus, you smell good."

She grinned. "You're doing better, then?"

"I haven't gotten to tell you one thing I can taste." He jammed his poles in the snow and cupped her cheeks. Capturing her soft mouth with his, he lost himself in her for a few seconds. In the way their kiss locked like a puzzle. In the way whatever she'd slicked on her lips was quickly becoming his favorite flavor.

"Chocolate," he stated, pulling away.

Eyes glossy and mouth parted, she blinked. "Huh?"

"One thing I taste."

"Oh. Right. My lip balm. You okay now?"

"I think so. Thanks for being so in tune."

She blinked again, a little irritation among the confusion. "I read energy for a living, Caleb."

A decade and a half of medical training wanted to roll its eyes hard, but he wasn't going to be a dick, not while she was being so understanding.

Didn't matter if he didn't buy all the nitty-gritty theory of what she did—she was still compassionate and ridiculously skilled with people. He didn't feel embarrassed about his anxiety, either. In practice, he tried not to— hard to convince his patients to accept their mental health struggles if he couldn't do the same with his own—but something about being with an alluring woman brought out the caveman in him. Made him feel he should be infallible. Well, screw that. She didn't seem to need it, and he obviously wasn't able to fake it. "You're amazing."

Her smile went soft at his compliment. "You say that and you haven't even seen me ski yet."

"Sure I have—watched you come down the hill before we went for lunch the other day. You have skills, Gem."

She shook her head. "I like Sharky better."

"I just like you."

Her jaw went a little slack.

Ah, crud. Too much, Matsuda. First, you freak out, then—

"I like you, too." Fixing her goggles in place, she slid away backward, a smirk creeping up her cheeks. She looked fully relaxed for the first time all day. With a neat turn, she pointed downhill and called out, "Race you to the bottom!"

And he slid forward for the first time in almost two years, trying not to think too closely about how he was pretty sure he'd follow her anywhere.

Thighs burning, Caleb bolted down a tricky mogul run. *Way to overcommit, idiot.* It figured Garnet's favorite run would be a double black diamond—expert level. The steep pitch and large bumps of Hammond's Chute pushed his muscles to their limit.

The morning had gone well enough that he'd reminded Garnet he used to ski extreme terrain and asked her for an after-lunch challenge. He didn't train specifically to ski anymore, but he'd taken up CrossFit after the avalanche, which kept him ready for pretty much anything. Even so, this run was a challenge. His knees faltered and he checked his technique. He could dig deep, show off a little.

Bail in front of a sexy woman and you'll never forgive yourself.

Halfway down the slope already, barely breathing hard, she waited for him, all mesmerizing joy and strong female physicality. She leaned forward on her poles, stretching her calves in alternating lunges.

He stopped, showering her with snow.

"Hey! Violation!" she complained lightly, wiping the snow from her goggles.

"Nope. Fair play. You failed to mention your favorite run is as bumpy as a bad case of poison ivy."

Her mouth quirked. "You're handling it fine."

"Classic fake it till you make it. My legs are ready to fall off."

"Good excuse for a hot tub later."

"Now that's motivation to finish the rest of this damned run."

Her jaw relaxed, a small admission which his libido wanted to label as desire in a bad way. "That it is. Saw one on your deck the other day and got ideas."

He pretended surprise. "Ms. James, are you inviting yourself over for après-ski?"

"I was promised breakfast."

"I promised a whole lot more than breakfast." His groin tightened, and he looked down the crazy vertical to cool off. "Provided we make it down alive."

Her mouth, a moue of desire, cracked with a hint of regret.

"What?"

She bit her lip. "Nothing. Let's finish the run."

He chased her down the last half, curiosity over her obvious lie burning in his chest to match his searing legs.

He'd prod her about it more once they got to the bottom, but he needed to focus on keeping pace with the Energizer Bunny: Winter Edition.

This run took technique and guts, and she had both in spades. A poetic, alpine masterpiece. The innate rhythm, even and smooth like a slow heartbeat. Deceiving the eye, making it look simple.

Every straining muscle in his body shouted that good grief, there was nothing simple or easy to be found on this particular slope.

He was so going to need the hot tub she'd mentioned, along with a handful of ibuprofen and a glass or two of wine.

He caught an edge on the top of a mogul, and his knees jolted to his chest. Damn it. Ow.

Wine wasn't going to cut it. This abuse demanded liquor. The bottle of high-end Japanese whisky his grandfather had sent him for his birthday last year, to be specific.

A few more teeth-rattling turns—his knees were going to hate him tomorrow, whiskey or not—and he was at Garnet's side. Sweat dripped down his temples, but damn, he felt good. Nothing but surgery could amp him up like a challenging run, and his blood sang with adrenaline, with the victory of having made it out intact.

Maybe the avalanche hadn't stolen as much from him as he thought.

It took your friends. And your ability to operate.

His gut twisted. Not exactly time for celebration, no matter how much he managed to get back on the alpine horse.

Garnet stroked his arm, the leather of her glove rasping against the waterproof material of his jacket. "No way you should be looking so serious after showing Hammond's who's boss. You thinking about Zach?"

"Huh? No... Why?"

"That's the run he fell on this past spring."

Caleb scanned back up to the top of the run and swore. "And he made it out with only a broken femur? Lucky bastard."

"His arm, too. But still."

"Could have been way worse." How many times had people said that to him after the avalanche? Daily for a while, there. Zach had probably dealt with it doubly, following both the slide and his separate job site accident. But where Zach was all done with his rehab and back to work, Caleb was still not functioning like he'd hoped. *Until you forgive yourself, you won't be able to move on.* His therapist's words. But the guy was wrong. Caleb didn't need to forgive himself for the avalanche— he hadn't caused it.

But he could forgive himself for feeling glad that he survived...

No. Processing that was impossible, let alone finding peace with it.

He swallowed. "I wouldn't have gone down it had I known it was where Zach broke his leg."

Guilt flickered in her eyes.

"And that's why you didn't tell me before."

"I—" She stared at the tips of her skis. "I wanted to prove to you there was no reason for you not to enjoy being on a mountain again."

"I have a hell of a reason, Garnet." A crack split down his chest. The only reason he could physically manage skiing was that it didn't involve too much precision from his fingers. "And some days, that reason might override my desire to get up here. Today, though? Not one of those days." He pressed his lips together and gestured to the lift far off in the distance at the bottom of the easier run that Hammond's Chute fed into. "You want me to prove something? Fine. Let's hit up some trees next."

An hour later and Garnet was pretty sure Caleb was ready to fall over. His legs had to be gassed. She caught his wince as they sat on the lift that would take them to the top of the gondola.

There weren't any runs down to the base on that face of the mountain, so they'd have to download from mid-station. After a day of skiing harder than usual, she knew her own legs weren't upset, either, about losing out on a little more vertical.

Caleb took his poles in one hand and looped his arm around her as he'd been doing on every lift. Though since Hammond's Chute it felt like his shadows had been chasing them, flitting in and out of the trees in the East Glade, tagging on their heels as they finished off on one of the more popular blue trails.

He still had his goggles on, so she couldn't tell if those shadows had settled into his eyes. The grim set of his lips would suggest yes.

She stuck her poles under her thigh and slid off her helmet, resting her head on his shoulder. The thin beanie she wore under her helmet would keep her ears warm enough until they got to Creekview.

"Nap time?" he murmured, warm breath brushing her cheek, fending off the cold wind for a few seconds.

"I don't know what you're talking about," she said, yawning.

He kissed the top of her head. "Could get used to cuddling you on a chairlift."

"I've made my point, then."

He made some sort of noncommittal, frustrated-man noise.

She opened her mouth to protest, but caution grabbed the words back. He'd worked through a lot today. And just because he was good with skiing today didn't mean he would be every day. She'd learned that mental health required pauses and shifts in the journey.

You have needs, too. Don't forget that.

She wouldn't. She'd spent too long learning it—had found herself in ugly places, like getting insulted by Bryce, or waking up with a ripping hangover and her freaking face on a friend's toilet seat—to forget now.

But she still wasn't convinced Caleb was in this for the right reasons. She couldn't shake free of having connected his desire to fit in with his desire to date her. No matter that he'd been saying all the right things today—years of not feeling good enough made it hard to trust.

Neither of them said much for the rest of the ride up or as she fetched her backpack from where she'd left it in the Creekview patrol shack. He took the bag from her and put it on his shoulders. Unnecessary chivalry, though she wasn't going to complain.

"Is everything, uh, ready for the party on your end? Friday's coming fast," she asked, setting the combination lock on the door.

He shuffled on his skis. "You mean with organizing music and finalizing the menu, or with my head?"

She shrugged noncommittally.

"Everything's under control. My list's all crossed off, and I'm pretty sure if I can ski a double black, I'll be okay going up the chairlift for dinner."

Ugh, why couldn't she have that confidence?

"What's next, Sharky?"

God, who knew? She could either ignore her overriding worry and jump his bones tonight, or she could talk to him.

And hopefully still jump his bones.

But first, adulting. Which they needed privacy for.

They joined the short gondola download line, and she caught the operator's eye. Harman was a seasonal employee in his early twenties.

"Yo, G-Jam!" he called from his perch.

She glanced back at the line. Not too long. Maybe she'd throw her employee status around for once. *Solo trip?* she mouthed at Harman.

He shot finger guns at her. "You got it, baby doll. Merry Christmas."

Caleb's palm landed on her belly and pulled her back against him.

So they were at the marking territory stage? Interesting development. She wasn't sure how to feel about that. Her painstakingly built independent side stiffened, well-tuned to any signs of sliding into a relationship where she wasn't on equal footing. But some primal part of her liked the possession. And as long as he was willing to be equally claimed by her, she could dial it back a little.

They shuffled forward, plastered together. The movement was hella awkward, given they were both carrying their skis and poles.

"I'm not sure what to laugh at the most," he said, bending to her ear. "G-Jam? Or the cheesy finger point."

She waved at Harman as he held up the line so that she and Caleb could get on the car by themselves. "I'm not going to be too hard on the guy. He's dealing with grief from the foursome behind us in line so that we could be total assholes and get the car to ourselves."

The doors thudded shut and Caleb glanced around the otherwise-empty, six-person space. A hint of mischief cracked through the weariness she knew he'd been wearing like a cloak. "This car's got a broken seat," he said, quoting the excuse the liftie had spouted to the crowd.

"You got it, baby doll," she mimicked, pressing a finger to the middle of Caleb's chest until he sloughed her backpack and sat on one of the benches. The car rocked a little, rising and falling over the top tower.

"Caleb?"

"Yeah?" he murmured, pulling her to kneel over his lap.

"Are you just interested in me because you want to make more friends in town?"

Blinking rapidly, he drew back as much as he could, given the closeness of her straddling his thighs. "What?"

"You mentioned wanting that yesterday. And I started to worry—" she resisted nibbling on the inside of her cheek "—that you wanted to be with me for the same reason."

His jaw hung a little loose. "No. Absolutely not."

She swallowed down the instinct not to believe him and rested a hand on his chest. "Okay, then."

"Why would you think that?"

"Relationship scars," she admitted.

"Garnet…" His throat bobbed. "If anything, I'm worried this won't work, and everyone will hate me because I broke your heart."

"Don't break my heart, then."

"Confession time, though—my ex was a real outdoor thrill seeker. And when I couldn't do that anymore… Things fell apart between us. I don't want that to happen with you."

She drew a lazy line along the zipper of his undershirt. "Look, I'd have a hard time dating someone who doesn't ski at all. For the sheer fact that during the winter I spend most of my spare time on the hill. But I don't need you to be my mirror. I just need you to be okay with me being me."

A smile cracked his seriousness. "I like you a hell of a lot."

Warmth cascaded through her body, and she held her palms over what had to be pink cheeks.

"Noticed something at lunch today." He dragged a thumb along her lower lip.

She nipped at his thumb, eliciting a groan. "What's that?"

"You don't have a bib on your ski pants."

"And?"

"And that could end really well for you."

She unclipped his helmet and set it on the seat beside them. "We have whatever's left of thirteen minutes— eight, maybe? And we're wearing way too much clothing."

"A challenge, then."

He kissed the heck out of her—her limbs went limp. So that was actually possible? Who knew?

And before she could figure out a way to get back at him for stripping her of her senses in under a minute, he spun her on his lap until her back pressed to his front and her legs draped over the outsides of his thighs.

He stroked her cheek with the backs of his fingers and dragged her jacket zipper open with his other hand.

Slowly.

"If you're actually going to get anything accomplished before we reach the base, you're going to have to speed up," she complained. The position, knowing she was letting him fully take charge, made her pulse race. Desire pooled in her belly, and she squirmed in his lap, wanting to feel something, anything, at her core.

"You're hell on a man's confidence, you know that?"

His tone was playful enough she didn't think her

complaints had actually wounded his ego. She dropped her head back on his shoulder and turned her face inward, kissing his jaw where skin met stubble. "Prove me wrong."

"With pleasure." Parting her jacket, he sneaked a hand under her shirt, skimming it upward until his palm cupped her breast over her sports bra.

She whimpered and shifted in his lap again. Pleasure was right. Blood rushed in her ears, competing with the buzzing cable of the gondola.

Drawing a slow circle around her fabric-covered nipple, he let out a raspy chuckle. His other palm, warm and rough and big, rested on the bare flesh of her lower belly. "You're wiggling. Restless, maybe?"

"Maybe."

His thumb circled her nipple. "I can't get at these well enough without stripping you naked, but this…" He slid his pinky and ring finger under the waistband of her ski pants. "This seems more accessible."

"Leggings, though. And underwear."

"All things—" his fingers dipped under the elastic of her leggings "—I can get around. That what you want?"

An empty ache throbbed at the apex of her thighs, begging for his hand to sneak just a bit lower. Just enough to cover her with those callused fingers and trigger what would likely be the fastest release she'd had in years. God, she was too needy to care about seeming desperate. "Please."

"Such manners." Sliding his hand from her breast, he palmed her abdomen and held her secure, then used his knees to spread her legs wider.

A burst of heat flooded her center and she moaned. "All manners and anything ladylike are going to disappear but quick if you don't fricking touch me."

"I don't want ladylike." His fingers traveled another inch lower, toying with the trimmed hair on her mound. "I want you authentic. Loud, quiet, laughing, crying…"

"Caleb," she said between gritted teeth. The gondola lurched as it went over another tower. If they got to the bottom before he actually followed through on his promise, she'd weep. "I can be all of those things if you'd shift your fingers an inch toward the floor."

"An inch?" His fingers followed instructions but went no farther, parting the very top of her folds, a breath away from her aching bud.

"I should have known a doctor would be as literal as hell!"

She felt his smile against her cheek. "And I should have known how much fun you'd be to tease."

Grinding her hips in an attempt to get him to thrust his hand all the way into her heat, she gripped the outside of his thighs. "Cale…"

"Yeah, I know." Nudging her legs apart even farther, he traced a torturous, brilliant path through her center until his fingers were buried in her. Filling the aching void.

"Finally," she moaned.

Massaging her nub with his thumb and stroking a slow pace with his fingers, he mumbled, "Should've waited until I had you in my bed."

"Incorrect. This needed to happen now." She pushed against his hand, trying to get his touch deeper, harder, closer. The thread of her arousal pulled taut.

She'd break soon. Her breath caught, a fragment of fear among the kaleidoscope of desire casting fractured light into her body.

How easy would it be to lose a part of herself to him?

His hand tightened on her belly and his fingers sped up their sensuous rhythm. "You can let go. I've got you."

Her cry filled the gondola and she arched in his lap. She squeezed her eyes shut and dissolved on his hand, the burst of intensity leaving her breath short and her skin tingling and her mind racing.

His fingers had been fantastic.

But it was his words that did her in.

She wanted him to have her, to keep learning to let go with him. But did she know how to do that without hurting them both?

Chapter Ten

Caleb made his way to Garnet's townhouse just after six that night, trying to ignore the nagging feeling that he'd messed up somehow. After she'd dissolved in his lap in the gondola, they'd had to rush to straighten up before they got to the base. A few quick kisses later and she'd texted him her address, told him to come over for dinner and hurried away through the snow-covered town square.

It had seemed a whole lot like running away. But then, she had invited him over. Maybe he was overthinking it. And he was looking forward to getting a look at her space. He knocked. A faint "come in!" rang through the door.

He entered and toed out of his boots. "Garnet?" Her skis leaned against the wall beside a narrow table housing an overflowing ceramic bowl. He smiled at the heap of lip balm, old shopping lists, house keys and change. She had a habit of emptying her pockets here. Cute. And the place smelled amazing. Oregano and garlic and butter and a hint of her herbal shampoo.

"Welcome." She walked down the short hall toward him, hips swaying and smile easy. Affection spread through his chest and he leaned in for a sweet but overwhelming kiss. Drawing back, he mumbled, "You taste like dessert again."

"Hot chocolate flavor. Marisol bought it for me at this Canadian tea store she's addicted to." She scanned him from what had to be hat head to his sock feet, appreciation lighting her eyes. "I like Casual Caleb."

"I figured it wouldn't be a dress-up occasion."

She stroked her hand down his chest, and his chest muscles flinched. "We should not dress up more often. You look hot in a T-shirt."

So did she.

Quirking a smile at the desire spreading across her face, he traced the loose neckline of her own T-shirt, then ran a hand down her side to where the hem cut off low on her hips. "You essentially saw me in one at lunch—what's the difference?"

"None. You looked crazy hot then, too."

"Likewise." He cleared his throat and followed her down the short hall into her living area, which ran from a sitting room in the front through a dining space and back into a galley kitchen. His sock feet sank into a plush area rug. Her eclectic, colorful decorating style stopped the wood-paneled walls from seeming oppressive. She'd sprinkled the chalet-style architecture with personal twists—potted orchids, colorful throws, a set of antique skis hanging above the fireplace—and it came off so intrinsically her that he knew he could spend some good long minutes studying all the little details.

She held out her hands. "Well, this is where I spend my free time."

"In that chair, I bet." He gestured to the corduroy armchair by the window. A reading lamp curved over the back and books overflowed on the adjacent low wooden table. Frames with pictures of friends and international destinations were tucked into the shelves of a massive bookcase, in among a selection of fiction and nonfiction. Across the room, under the wood-plank mantle of the fireplace, she'd built a fire in the hearth. The crackling blaze warmed the room in both temperature and atmosphere.

"Recent renovation?" He motioned at what looked like new slate footings and stonework.

"Yeah." She twisted her hands. "One of the reasons I rent the place. I love having a cozy fire."

"And I love the idea of getting to snuggle with you in front of it."

"Want to eat dinner in here? I set the table, but…" She wrung her fingers hard enough to turn them white.

"Hey." He drew close, covering her hands with one of his. "What's on your mind?"

When she tilted her chin to look at him, worry marked her velvety gray irises. "Been a while since I've had a guy in my place."

And since she'd let one into her heart, too? She'd hinted at that. Damn, for all he could list the reasons why he shouldn't, he wanted to earn his way in. "It's cozy and full of personality."

"That's what I was going for."

He narrowed his eyes. Something about talking about her place was eroding her confidence, and he didn't like that. He kissed her softly, tried to coax the stiffness from her lips. "Where'd my sparky Sharky go?"

She shook her head, one of those exaggerated clearing-thoughts gestures. "Somewhere I usually aim to avoid."

"Well, come back to me." He linked his arms around her waist and sat on the couch, pulling her down with him. She tucked into his side, legs draped over his lap. "I was feeling hard done by, not being able to shower off the day with you."

"Was?"

"Yeah. Decided I'll make it up by showering off the night instead."

She clenched a fistful of his shirt. "I see."

"In the morning," he clarified. "We'll shower off the night in the morning."

"Yeah, got that." Her words came out breathy, strained. She kissed his jaw.

An urge rose to dive in, to lay her on the couch and carefully alternate removing her clothing and driving her to the brink. But his gut nudged him to be cautious. She'd been hesitant for a minute, and that deserved attention.

"We don't have to decide about the morning until we see how the night goes," he suggested.

"I invited you here, didn't I?" Taking his hand, she turned it palm up and traced the insides of his fingers one at a time. She didn't trace his scars, but she didn't avoid them, either. Hopefully she felt the same way about the ones on the inside, too.

"It was a hasty invitation," he pointed out.

Her eyes crinkled with lighthearted guilt. "I was a little overwhelmed. My brain shorted out. Sorry for splitting on you like that."

"Surprised you invited me over, then. You could have come to my place, given yourself the ability to leave if you needed to."

In the middle of fidgeting with his fingers, playing a mock piano on the tips, she paused. "I owed you dinner."

He tightened his arm around her back. "You don't owe me anything. I just want to enjoy your company."

A deep sigh shuddered through her body. "Yeah?"

"The fire, ski-sore muscles, sitting like this—I don't need much else."

"Truth."

"Except maybe some garlic bread."

And fewer articles of clothing.

But he could be patient.

* * *

Caleb leaned back in his chair and groaned, linking his hands over his flat stomach, and Garnet couldn't help but grin.

"Overfed and out of energy? I think you're trying to ruin me," he groused.

"Poor baby. And here I thought the night was just beginning."

His mouth twitched. "I'm a stereotypical guy, Garnet. Give the word, and I'll spring back to life."

"Literally?"

He snorted. "Literally."

"Excellent."

A hunger entirely unrelated to food crossed his face, followed by a wince. "Well, five minutes to digest first. That gnocchi was good enough to bring Jamie Oliver to his knees."

"Thanks. Though I'd rather have you at my mercy."

"Oh, you will."

Temptation curled in her belly. Who cared about the dishes or being tired and achy from their hard day on the slopes?

The possibility of straddling this man again, him using his tongue instead of his fingers, overshadowed all of that. Overshadowed everything.

But if he wanted five minutes, she supposed she could wait.

A pang of impatience shot up her spine and she swallowed. "We can deal with the sink full of dishes while you recuperate."

"Let's not get carried away with the monotonous, now. Handwashing's for chumps. My dishwasher-loading skills are exceptional."

And he proved that, lining up the plates, pots and pans with precision and speed.

He stood at the sink washing his hands, and she came up behind him and rubbed slow fingertips along his lats. "What other exceptional skills do you have?"

"I didn't answer that question in the gondola?" He shut off the water and dried his hands on the tea towel on the counter.

She laughed and pressed harder into his back muscles. They were tight, probably giving him some mild grief. "I guess you did."

"Gigi, are you—"

"Gigi?" she interrupted, blinking in surprise.

"That's a no, too?" He frowned. "Man, I am striking out."

"No… It's fine, actually. I just wasn't expecting it." But she liked it, both the name, and his insistence he find something unique to call her.

"Mmm, good. Question—are you going to be annoyed if I ask you to do whatever you're doing to my back some more?"

"It's just a massage, Caleb."

"A real one?"

She stilled her hands. *Real.* The word sank like a brick, tugging at the back of her throat. "What do you mean, real?"

He turned slowly. Stricken regret pulled at the corners of his mouth. "I didn't mean it that way."

She crossed her arms and backed up until her hips hit the opposite counter. "Didn't you?"

"No. God, no."

"It's what you implied when we first met up to plan the party." Not wanting to see disapproval replace his regret, she squeezed her lids shut.

"Garnet."

The plea in his voice pried her eyes open. He stood in front of her with his hands at his sides, fingers outstretched as if he was trying not to touch her. Nothing but earnest apology rode his handsome features.

She relaxed her flattened lips, but nerves made her jaw jut out in the process. "I won't be with someone who looks down on what I do."

"Hey. Anyone who knows you and doesn't see how incredible you are is blind to reality."

"And you think you know me?"

"Yeah." The soft word shot through her heart like an archer's arrow. "I think I do."

Whether or not that was true? Irrelevant.

She wanted it to be true.

Wanted to open up enough of herself to him to make it true.

But really. How could he have figured her out so quickly when it had taken herself years to do the same? She couldn't trust his feelings. Not yet. She glanced to the side, focusing out the window over the sink instead of on his face. A light snow was falling, the sprinkling of flakes caught in her back porch light. A few larger clumps joined the dusty swirl.

"Snow's getting heavier." Her voice was tight, and she didn't bother to hide it.

He jammed his hands in his pockets and rocked back on his heels. "I should drive home before I get stuck here, in other words?"

She shook her head and dropped her gaze to his feet instead of the window. "We still have a fire to enjoy. Unless you have to get up early for work."

"I don't work Mondays. You?"

"Not until noon."

"So let's enjoy the fire. No need to overthink things." He cupped her cheek with a gentle hand. "Got any chestnuts to roast?"

The corny reference gave her pause, and she snorted. She looked up at him. "Does anyone actually do that?"

"No earthly idea. Definitely not at my grandparents' place in Brooklyn. We have fried chicken for my grandfather, and my granny—she's Welsh—makes teeth-cracking Christmas cake. It's almost edible if you dunk it in mulled wine." He chuckled. "Thankfully, she's better at making that than baking."

Garnet smiled. "I'm the baker in my family. I need to make a few pies next week, actually. I'm working on Christmas Day—might as well let the people with small kids have the day off—but Mom and Dad are still counting on me to bring the usual for dinner."

"Which is?"

"One spiced cherry, one eggnog meringue."

He shot her a dubious expression.

"Trust me, they're both delicious."

Shuffling his feet, he leaned back against the sink. "Big crowd for dinner, then?"

"Just the three of us. Most of the pie goes uneaten, but my dad likes variety."

Guilt crept up her neck. Should she invite Caleb along? *Holy crackers, are you crazy? Too soon. Not happening.*

"My extended family's in California," she explained, rushing to fill the silence. "We've lived here for decades because my parents work at the university in Bozeman, but no one else likes to leave the Bay Area."

"That's okay. Holidays don't need to be a big thing. Small gatherings can be just as meaningful as large ones."

"Small, like two people?" she mused, then regretted her lack of filter.

"Exactly." He squinted his eyes in thought. "Got any barbecue skewers?"

"At the back of a drawer somewhere."

"And marshmallows?"

She liked where this was going. "Yeah…"

"Those are better to roast than chestnuts any day."

Twenty minutes later they sprawled on the rug in front of the fireplace, even more stuffed after their impromptu s'mores-roasting session.

Setting her skewer on a plate on the coffee table, she snuggled up to Caleb. He lay flat on his back, eyes heavy-lidded and smile lazy. He banded a strong arm around her back.

"You have chocolate—" she rose up on an elbow "—*riiiight* here." With a flick of her tongue, she caught the dab at the corner of his mouth.

Eyes darkening, he turned his head. His lips were on hers and before she could process anything other than the sweetness of his tongue and the smoky desire cresting on his face, he had their positions flipped.

"Didn't want me on top?" she squeaked.

"We've got plenty of time for whatever suits your fancy."

The possibilities bloomed through her body. She melted into the rug a little. "Mmm."

"But this is a good place to start, don't you think?"

"What I think, Caleb…" His hand skimmed up her stomach, stealing her ability to speak. She cleared her throat. "What I think—"

He cupped her breast, thumb circling her nipple, and the rush of pleasure flooded from her skin to her center.

She moaned. Her fingers dug into his back. How the

hell did it feel so intense? She was wearing a bra and T-shirt, for God's sake.

Her nipple didn't care. It pebbled under his ministrations.

He dipped his head to her breast, mouthing the place he'd aroused so quickly. "What is it you think?"

"That you should take off my shirt."

Complying in a smooth motion, he tossed the garment onto the armchair. His mouth settled back on her nipple. Her thin bra did nothing to mute the sensation of teeth scraping tender skin. The damp material only added friction, heightening her pleasure. He moved to the other side and captured the other nipple between smiling lips.

That smile.

Not so lazy anymore. A cocky awareness flickered at the corners, matching the glint in his deep brown eyes. "What else do you think?"

She tugged at the hem of his T-shirt. "That you should take off *your* shirt."

The gray cotton landed over hers on the chair.

Though it could have landed in the fireplace and she wouldn't have noticed. Damn, Caleb was cut. And his skin was perfectly warm, with just enough hair on his chest to make things interesting.

He brushed her hair from her forehead and locked gazes with hers. With a steady hand, he worked the clasp of her bra free and slid the straps off her arms. Pupils flaring, he added it to the pile, followed by her leggings. His belt buckle was cool on the skin at her waist, contrasting with the warmth from the fire. "And now?"

"We can probably stop thinking, don't you think?"

"Something tells me your brain's always going."

She huffed out a breath, but it was hard to be offended when:

a) it wasn't really an insult, and;

b) he was right.

"Says the know-it-all doctor," she retorted, though her tone lacked oomph.

He licked a path down her jaw to her collarbone. His breath cooled the hot, damp trail, and her skin shivered.

Desire pulsed at her core. She wanted his hands on her again, delving into her wetness. Hell, she wanted her hands on him, too.

The anticipation of the first touch spun in her blood, a heady, dizzy awareness. Tension crackled in her veins, snapping with flame like the logs in the grate. Good thing she was lying down.

She reached for his belt buckle, fumbling with the metal fastening, and explored his flat belly. Two fingers just below the elastic of his boxers.

His eyes shuttered closed, and a groan rattled from his lungs. The air teased the skin at her collarbone, then her nipple as he licked her flesh. The ensuing frisson of need was all the motivation she needed to reach in and palm his erection.

"Good to know you want this as much as I do," she murmured.

He mouthed her skin and let out a muffled string of profanity.

She slowly stroked his length. "No need to get so negative about it," she teased. "Aren't we supposed to be having fun here?"

"Garnet." He shifted between her legs, settling everything hard exactly where she wanted it.

She let out her own curse, thrusting against him.

Dark need filled his eyes and breath sawed in and out of his chest. He'd be gorgeous on an off day. But knowing the craving in his eyes was for her, that he wanted to get closer to her and experience as epic a release as they could manage? A damned heady turn-on. And one she wasn't entirely sure she was ready for.

"I'm just saying you're not the only person here who's figured some things out about the other. And you—" She nipped at his mouth. His stubble rasped her cheek. She'd have some serious whisker burn by the morning and it would be awesome. "You have the tendency to get serious."

"I do." He circled his hips, grinning as she whimpered. "I will always take getting you off very, very seriously."

"A promise?"

"A damned vow, Garnet."

She melted into the carpet, and her eyes shuttered half-closed. "What a freaking sweet talker."

Shrugging, he rose up to shuck off his pants and boxers, taking a condom from his pocket and sheathing himself.

"And prepared, too," she said.

"Comes with the job description." His mouth lifted into a half smile.

"I'm on the Pill. We have backup."

"Good call." He knelt between her legs, settling back on his heels. His hands traced teasing patterns on her inner thighs and he inched his thumbs closer to her sex. Closer, closer, until the tips of his fingers traced the edge of her simple panties, then stilled.

Crap. Should she have worn something sexier? Thing was, she didn't have lace. Seamless microfiber was as good as it got. Could have gone to buy a new pair, though. Getting naked had been inevitable, and… Just crap. She chewed on her lip and stared at him.

His gaze was going a little hazy. Mouth open, his tongue flicked out and wet his lower lip. He downright consumed her from face to thighs with a hungry look. "You are so beautiful."

"You too," she said on a breath. She rubbed her feet against his calves. The hair tickled her soles. He was the perfect amount of masculine. But hard calves and roughened hands and built shoulders, though candy for the senses, didn't satiate all her cravings.

"Caleb?"

"Yeah?"

"Move your fingers."

He grinned. "Where?"

"You know where." She wriggled her hips, rubbing her ass against his knees.

"You'll have to tell me."

"Take my panties off, Caleb."

A flick and slide, and they were gone. He started teasing her again, slow, light touches that threatened to light her on fire.

She grabbed his wrist and pulled.

The corners of his eyes crinkled as he covered her. The weight of him, heavy on her torso… "Holy crap. I never want you to move. Ever."

He touched his forehead to hers, kissing her softly. Sliding his hand between their bodies, he cupped her sex. A finger slid between her folds and her muscles pulsed. "Ever?"

She laughed, but then he thrust his finger deeper, cutting off the sound.

She couldn't even think when he did that with his hand, let alone make noises that weren't base, sexual moans.

"Oh," she cried.

Firelight flickered alongside the humor and passion in his eyes. "So you *want* me to move," he rasped.

Wrapping her legs around his hips, she tried to make her agreement clear.

"I want you too much," she murmured. She'd probably regret that admission later, but with the soft rug at her back and the weight of him at her front and his erection so very close to taking her everywhere she wanted to go, she couldn't bring herself to care.

His lips pressed into hers, and his stubble tickled the already abraded skin around her mouth. "Want you, too. Now."

And with a swift stroke, he proved that, filling her, tearing a cry from her throat.

He swore again, a low, raspy curse. All traces of their earlier laughter were gone.

The slow, measured rhythm consumed her until the crackling of the fire grew faint under the rush of blood in her ears. Her impatient hips searched, snapping higher and harder against him.

Their mouths mimicked the mad movements of their bodies. She was so close. But she ached to get that much closer. "Touch me. I need your hand, too."

He complied, toying with her sensitive bud until her world narrowed to that tiny knot of bliss and the way he filled her body.

She dug her nails into his shoulders and her back arched and it was close to heaven but not quite, not quite... The pool of arousal spilled over, waves rocketing to her toes and fingers. She shouted something. Who the hell knew what? Her ears weren't working anymore. He thrust deep and groaned his own pleasure. Another rush tore through her, an overwhelming, lush aftershock. She clung to him.

Her fingers weakened on his skin, failing to find purchase. Every muscle in her body went limp. "Caleb..."

Damp hair tickled her cheek as he shook his head, which he'd buried in her shoulder at some point—maybe when he'd found his release? Time had blurred.

Letting her arms fall to the ground like a rag doll, she mumbled his name again.

"Sorry, yeah, I'll move." With a hand to his groin—good he was thinking about the condom, because she'd forgotten about it—he rolled to the side, then rested his arm on her belly.

"It's okay. I like your weight on me."

"Same."

His eyes were closed, head tipped back a little. The slowing of his breathing rate caught her attention. The privilege of watching him relax after something so intimate was almost more private than the original act.

And panic teased the edges of her consciousness again. No turning back now.

"You, uh, want that massage you asked for earlier?" she asked.

"I'm not sure I still have a body after what we just did." His mouth curved against her shoulder. "I can't feel it, so it must not exist."

"Oh, it exists." She drew circles in the hair on his chest. "Need proof of that?"

"Depends on the proof."

She nudged his shoulder until he rolled on his front. "Give me ten minutes. I'll make up for cheating you out of a hot tub tonight. And once you're relaxed and happy…"

He caught her hand with his and turned his head to the side to kiss her fingers. "I couldn't be more relaxed and happy."

Chapter Eleven

Caleb woke up cocooned in Garnet's cozy bed, face-to-face with her. Their hands entwined between them on the flannel sheets. He tried to stay still, not wake her.

She suited the morning. They'd slept in long enough that the sun had chased away the winter dark, and light shining on her skin brought out the charming sprinkle of freckles on her nose and cheeks.

He'd be happy to watch her sleep for hours, but nature called. Reluctantly, he slid from the sheets. He took care of business and then brushed his teeth using the spare toothbrush she'd given him last night.

As he tiptoed back into her warmly decorated room his heart sank at the empty, rumpled covers. Damn. So much for languid snuggles.

He pulled on his boxers, but couldn't find his shirt. Stealing his clothes, was she? He'd have to show up for breakfast unsuitably dressed, then. Grinning to himself, he went searching for his woman.

Warning bells clanged at the territorial thought.

No. He fisted his hands. *It's okay—good, even—to be vulnerable, to feel this way again.*

And the sight of her, fumbling with her French press with her phone pinched between her shoulder and ear—that was good, too.

Her eyes were a sleepy gray, and as he suspected, his T-shirt graced her shoulders, hitting her at midthigh. She had a tattoo hidden under the cotton on her back. A dragonfly, with rich pinks, blues and purples bleeding out from black edges. He'd discovered it once he carried her to bed last night. And he'd be happy to explore it some more this morning.

He sidled up behind her, tugging on the hem and tucking her sweet ass into his front. "Looks better on you than me."

The comment earned him a light elbow to the solar plexus. He dropped his mouth to the exposed side of her neck and nuzzled close.

"Gotcha, Ryan," she said into the phone, voice hitching.

Ah, the sheriff. Top of the SAR food chain for the county, so long as jurisdiction was the same here as in Colorado. Geez, the guy was calling before nine on a Monday? Talk about dedicated to the job. Though Caleb couldn't point fingers. He'd be on call at the hospital for most of next week, including nights on the twenty-fourth and twenty-fifth, while everyone else spent Christmas with their families. He agreed with Garnet—might as well let the people with kids enjoy the holiday.

But seriously, Garnet had better things to do this morning than talk to her SAR team leader.

Mainly, Caleb himself.

He scraped his teeth along her shoulder, and she yelped quietly. "Yeah, I'm on the hill extra next week."

A pause.

"I know, hopefully we don't get a Christmas call like last year. My parents don't live far, though. I'll have my app on."

A Christmas call. As in her, grappling down a gully or up an icy slope, looking for someone who'd lost their bearings.

Or their life.

Caleb had to fight to keep his fingers from tightening on her hips. He tried to take a calming breath without drawing her attention.

She said goodbye and placed her phone on the counter. When she turned, concern filled her gaze.

She palmed his chest and stroked a soothing rhythm. "Something triggering you?"

"Just a lack of coffee." His fear about her SAR work was his problem. It wasn't fair for him to put his issues on her. So until he figured out how to be good with her being out on rescues, he'd keep quiet.

A knot of disbelief formed between her brows. "You sure?"

"Sure I need coffee? Yeah. You kept me up half the night."

Stilling her circling palm, she drummed her fingers against his pec. She sighed, a resigned look crossing her face. After a beat, an unapologetic smirk tugged at her mouth. "I did do that."

He eased into a kiss. Took a minute to test her lips, for the mint of his toothpaste to mix with the creamy coffee flavor on her tongue. Her fingertips bit into his chest.

"It was the best night I've had in a long time," he said. "It's been a while since I've slept over at someone's place."

She cocked her head. "Bit of a dry spell?"

"I haven't dated since I split from Meiko."

"How long ago was that?"

"A couple months after the slide."

Shifting out of his grip, she reached into the cupboard for a mug, then poured from the French press. Her hand shook a little as she handed him the drink. "This feels like it could be significant if we let it."

He took the offering and leaned against the counter. "If that's what you want."

"It's about what you want, too."

Getting back the parts of himself he missed would be a start. And Garnet James co-opting his T-shirts for lazy-morning attire seemed the way to go about that. "I want more of this, Sharky. Waking up in your bed. Coffee. Sharing an omelet."

She braced a hand on her hip. "My omelet game is pitiful."

"Mine isn't." He took her hand and tugged her against his side.

She dipped her gaze somewhere in the vicinity of their bare toes. "I need to know you can handle my patrolling and my rescue work."

"I told you, I used to be trained in SAR."

"I know. But then…"

He tightened his arm around her and slugged his coffee. The too-big gulp seared the back of his throat. "I dealt with that."

The hum of the fridge rent the ensuing silence. After a long pause, she cleared her throat, and repeated, "You sure?"

He drew back far enough to question her with a raised brow. "You only get to ask me that once a morning."

"It just doesn't seem—"

"I'll let you know if there's something we need to work through." Putting his coffee down on the counter, he tipped up her chin with a finger. She seemed to take his doubts personally, so he wasn't going to embark on that craggy road this morning. No, kissing her seemed the way to go. Digging a hand into her hair, he massaged her mouth with his until he could feel her heart thudding against his chest. Until the drum of his own racing pulse was all he could hear in his ears.

Until the goose bumps on his skin were from her sweet fingers dancing on his back instead of from being shirtless on a December morning.

"Which scene of the crime are we revisiting?" he asked. "The fireplace, or your bed?"

"Neither." A naughty smile spread on her face. "I was promised a shower."

The morning of the party rolled around, a diamonds-and-white-velvet day after fresh snowfall. Garnet buzzed with energy. Excitement about the party, sure, but she had to be honest with herself—even five days after waking up with Caleb, she couldn't slough off the residual rush she'd gotten from his hands caressing her skin. She had spent the middle of the week juggling Evolve and patrolling shifts with a couple of evening drives to Bozeman to pick up decorations. Her one attempt at seeing Caleb since their Monday morning of omelets and sex had been a bust. She stared into her open refrigerator and sighed at the dinner leftovers. He had been on call last night at the hospital, and right when she'd gotten in from an out-of-bounds emergency on the hill that had kept her over her usual shift end, he'd been paged to deal with a woman in premature labor.

And by the grim scowl he'd worn on his way out the door, seemingly brought on by her admitting she'd tweaked her knee while pulling the rescue toboggan through the late-afternoon, tracked-out, garbage snow, he'd been happy for the excuse to leave.

He hadn't returned.

She gripped her coffee cup. Her knuckles creaked. He

sure as hell wasn't okay with the dangerous parts of her patrolling and rescue work.

I dealt with that. Coffee slopped onto her hand as she slammed the mug onto her counter.

As if.

She hated being lied to. But given they had to spend their afternoon decorating for the staff party, today probably wasn't the day to deal with it. She doubted she'd be able to shift her concerns aside entirely, though. Hard to ignore him being unhappy. Even harder to ignore how his unhappiness, if left to fester, meant they wouldn't succeed long term.

Disappointment panged in her throat. Hopefully it wouldn't come to that. Every part of him pulled her in— the seriousness with which he approached his work, the earnestness of wanting to be a part of the community, the humor that he brandished when he relaxed. And she wasn't going to complain about the orgasms…

Her phone chimed from the charging pad on the counter. She picked it up.

Caleb: I'm here till 8. Rescheduling morning appointments. Need nap.

He'd need breakfast, too. And after being up all night, he shouldn't drive home.

She sighed. Damn her overdeveloped concern for others' well-being. She had the day blocked off for party setup, so she could get him settled before she got to work on sorting all the decorations they'd ordered. With having to change his workday around, he probably wouldn't be able to help her as much as planned.

Might be for the better, given the mental picture of that scowl that she couldn't seem to shake.

But she wasn't going to let him be unsafe, either.

She typed a reply. Need a lift to wherever you're planning to nap?

A text bubble hung on the screen for a minute. Either he was writing an essay, or debating his answer.

Caleb: If it's not too much trouble.

Oh, he was trouble, all right. She really had to get a better picture of how her work affected his PTSD. Because she'd forgotten how fun it was to be infatuated with someone, and she'd started to enjoy the silly grin she got on her face every time she got to see him.

Grabbing last night's dessert out of the fridge—nothing made for a better breakfast than pie, and she'd done a trial run of her spiced cherry recipe—she filled two travel mugs with coffee and made her way to the hospital.

And when she was waved through to the ER waiting room and caught sight of Caleb, deep in conversation with a middle-aged couple, her heart skipped a beat.

The lines pulling at his eyes and mouth spoke of a man who'd been up all night making tough decisions, probably about whether to deliver a baby or medically stall labor in hopes of having his patient gestate for another few weeks. And yet his expression remained earnest, engaged with the people with whom he was speaking. So much so that he didn't notice she'd entered the room. She put the travel mugs and the bagged pie on an end table and sat in one of the thinly cushioned chairs ringing the long narrow room.

He talked with his hands as much as his voice, and was drawing on a clipboard intermittently. The couple followed his every word.

Doubt burned in her throat. Would she be able to show

him that the risks of going out-of-bounds and into the backcountry were worth connecting with people, helping them much like he did daily?

A minute later, he turned to leave. They locked gazes. Tired relief spread on his handsome features. He dug both hands into his hair and stared at her for a second.

She could shelve her worries for now. He looked ready to fall over. She closed the half-room distance between them. Palming his cheek, she ran her thumb along his jaw. "Hey there, Dr. Delicious."

He kissed her forehead. "Dr. Delicious?"

"Seems more appropriate than your other nickname. You don't look like you want to do anything except sleep right now."

Puzzlement crinkled his forehead. "Huh?"

"Dr. Do-Me," she clarified. "I mean, I'm game, but I'm good with you taking that nap first."

He groaned. "Cadie has a big mouth."

"And you're hot as hell. And very deserving of the pie I brought you."

He wrapped her in a hug. She soaked in the closeness and laid her cheek on his chest. Warmth spread through the plaid shirt he had on under his open doctor's coat. His clean, man-soap scent cut through the hospital smells of disinfectant and bad coffee. Contentedness settled in her marrow.

Deep and solid and—

Oh.

That was a lot of feelings right there.

Falling feelings.

Damn.

"I was not expecting pie," he said. "Wasn't expecting you, either. Not until your text, that is."

Nerves cramped in her belly. She knew he was talking

about the moment. But it applied to her life, too. Caleb had dropped into her existence, and trying to figure out how to make space for him wasn't a simple task.

She took a centering breath. "Anything else you need to finish up, or are you ready for your taxi service?"

"Nope, I'm all done."

After he gathered his coat and mumbled his love for the coffee she'd brought him, he hung the pie bag over a wrist and took her hand, weaving their fingers together. "I'm pissed I missed dinner last night, but you sure have a way of spoiling a guy."

"Wouldn't want you to become a statistic."

His face grayed. "Been there, done that."

She cringed. "Sorry."

"No need to apologize."

"Your bordering-on-nausea look—" she circled a hand, indicating his face "—would suggest otherwise."

"I'm just tired." He dropped her hand and jammed his into his coat pocket, speeding up a little as he headed for the automatic doors. She followed as best she could, but her knee pinched with the reminder that she'd twisted it yesterday.

His face darkened. "That still bugging you?"

"It's seriously minor."

Her claim earned her a sleepy, unconvinced grunt. The doors slid open. Wind blasted them, and Caleb hunched his shoulders. "Since when do the patrollers become the casualties?"

"Caleb…" She tried to keep her tone level. "It happens. Just like any workplace injury. If it makes it any better, it's the first time I've been hurt on the job. SAR or patrolling. And if it's still bothering me tomorrow, I'll get it checked out."

He raked his hands through his hair, setting the thick strands into disarray. "No, it really doesn't make it better."

She opened the doors to her SUV with the key fob. They climbed in. Caleb tipped his head back and closed his eyes. After starting the vehicle, she reached over and rubbed his thigh. "It's not that bad."

"Could have been," he muttered.

"But it wasn't." Her conscience poked at her—she couldn't play the avoidance game. That was one of the things that had caused problems with Bryce, her ignoring the early signs that he wanted her to change. And if Caleb was awake enough to push the issue of her knee, he was awake enough to hear her concerns. "You know, you said you were fine with my job, and my volunteering, but I'm worried you weren't telling the truth."

He crossed his arms. "Can we table that, Garnet?"

Frustration teased her skin. "No, I don't think we can."

"To be honest, I don't know how I feel." His terse tone walloped like a sledgehammer.

"So why did you say it was fine?"

"I thought I could handle it."

"Or you were trying to force past something you shouldn't ignore for the sake of making connections."

He wiped a hand down his face. "What, you're mad at me because I want to date you?"

"No, I'm mad at you because you're not being honest with me." *For pretending to like all of who I am.* A hot stripe tingled up her back. Pulling the car out of the hospital lot, she gripped the steering wheel, trying to funnel her anger into the faux-leather covering.

The corners of his mouth pinched. His eyes were still closed, and goddamn it, she wanted him to open them so that she could glare at him.

"I've had my share of boyfriends who I played the chameleon for," she said. "I don't need another one."

"Garnet." He pressed the pads of his fingers against his eyes. "Holy crap. I'm not asking you to change."

"But you weren't honest. You can't just pick and choose the parts of my life that you like and dislike."

A breath shuddered from his chest, followed by a quiet "I'm not going to be the same guy from before—don't want to be, in all honesty—but accepting I have a mental health disorder doesn't mean I need to be okay with feeling unfulfilled. I'm working on the parts of me that are holding me back."

"I know," she whispered. But the scars of getting burned still tugged and pulled, a constant reminder to be wary of who she trusted.

She stopped at the red light at the intersection just around the corner from her apartment. She could take him there. Squeeze in a nap together. But she just wasn't feeling like it right now. She turned toward the lake drive. "If you lied about how you feel about my work, are you lying about feeling comfortable about attending the party?"

"I didn't—" He swore under his breath. "I'm not backing out on the party."

"Maybe you should," she whispered.

Pain flashed across his face. One of those flickers she still hadn't quite learned. Was it physical—such a long shift had to have left him with an aching arm—or emotional? Her heart cramped in sympathy.

"You don't want me to come?" he asked.

"I want you to be healthy. Safe," she murmured, letting go of the steering wheel with one hand and sliding her palm into his.

His fingers pulsed around hers. "Same."

"Maybe you should take a pause, then, not push yourself so hard." *Maybe we should take a pause.*

"Uh… I meant, same goes for you. I want *you* to be safe."

"And you don't think I am when I'm in the backcountry," she stated.

The silence went on too long, and when she looked away from the road, his eyes were closed.

"Caleb."

No response. Just the slow, steady cadence of his breathing.

Even her bark of disbelieving laughter didn't jar him from his slumber. *Oh, come on.*

Pulling up at his house a few minutes later, she shook his shoulder. *"Caleb."*

"Wha…?" He jolted straight.

"Take the pie." She forced a smile. "Have a good nap."

"Want to come join me?"

She stiffened at the suggestion in his tone, that he was completely overlooking their argument. "I have to organize stuff."

The corners of his mouth turned down. "I was supposed to help you."

And she'd been looking forward to it. Now? She didn't know. Her stomach twisted. "You'll meet me up at the lounge after it's closed for the day?"

"I'll be there," he said, leaning in for a kiss.

She accepted the touch, but couldn't quite manage to relax her lips. "If you're sure."

He stared at her. "Don't take your own uncertainty and shift it onto me, Gigi. I'm good with going up the mountain today. See you at four."

He slid out of the car and closed the door before she could protest.

What, he was going to blame *her*? How did this have anything to do with her?

You're being just as rigid as he was. Except now he's trying to adjust.

And you're not.

No. It wasn't the same.

But there was nothing quite like having her conscience hammering her with the similarities. It refused to shut up the rest of the afternoon, the entire time she was making contact with her vendors and arranging decorations into boxes to tow up the mountain behind a snowmobile.

By the time she had the boxes arranged around the Peak Lodge lounge and had given directions to the banquet staff on how to set up the tables, she was in serious need of a yoga class and some meditation.

Quiet footsteps approached on the industrially carpeted floor. "There a reason your shoulders are up by your ears, Sharky? Something not going right?" Her date, all six-plus feet of infuriating male, approached with a tentative smile. Droplets of water dotted his beanie; it must have started snowing sometime after her arrival up here. He shrugged out of a backpack and that infernally sexy charcoal wool coat she loved, and had a shirt and tie on underneath.

She wasn't planning on changing into her flirty cocktail dress until after they'd hung decorations. Nor was she going to get sucked in by how his dress pants put his ass in eighth-wonder-of-the-world territory. "It's been a busy day without you, but I've made good progress on the to-do list. Everything's fine."

Dropping his coat and bag onto the table next to the decorations, he cocked a brow. "Now who's lying?"

"I'm not going to hold your having worked through the night against you." She was madder at herself than anything, but no effing way was she going to admit that. Mad that she'd fallen for a guy who had her questioning everything she'd thought would protect her.

No. This was about him pointing out her rigidity, and he was wrong about that. If she softened, she might dissolve again. In her experience, there wasn't enough distance between compromising partner and weak push-over. She stomped across the room to the stone fireplace, grabbed one of the strings of white lights they'd bought and ripped into the packaging.

"I'm well aware my overnighter is not why you're pissed off." Caleb took a seat on the hearth and touched her elbow. He let out a long breath. "You've reeled me in. You're smart and sexy and funny. But everything about you, Garnet—there's risk involved. And I'm not good at risk anymore."

Her clamped jaw muscles released a bit at that. Well. There was the honesty she'd wanted.

And hearing it… Was it really better, having him confirm out loud that they weren't suited?

"You don't need to say anything," he said. "Just something to think about."

"And I will." It would probably be hard to think about anything else. Getting stuck in an ugly thought spiral was one of her greatest skills, after all.

This wasn't how today was supposed to have gone. She'd fooled herself that they were making progress. But arguing and struggling to be honest with each other? And him considering *her* risky? She didn't know where to file that.

And she really had to decide before she tumbled from infatuation into love.

Chapter Twelve

By ten that night, the party was in full swing. Caleb was willing to bet none of the other guests had to resort to cognitive behavioral therapy techniques to make it up the hill, but at least he'd arrived without sweating through his shirt. And the whirl of activity made it easy to ignore the fact he was going to have to take the gondola down in the dark. He deserved to enjoy the fruits of his labors. Well, partly his. Mostly Garnet's. But he'd hung twinkle lights and strewn the room with fancy paper snowflakes and three-dimensional cardboard trees. They'd kept it simple, and Garnet had been right—the high, pale-pine ceilings added to the festive ambience.

Not that he'd been able to pay much attention to anything but Garnet since the minute they'd finished decorating and she'd changed into her party dress. A column of jade silk draped her curves. The faint sheen of the fabric caught the light from the white lights draped on the mantle. Caught his attention, too. Beyond his eyes or the heat settling in his belly, her beauty sank a hook deep in his chest.

An awareness he hadn't felt since the start of his last relationship when he'd walked into a Brooklyn coffee shop, grumbling to himself about his grandfather's attempts to play matchmaker, and had gotten sucked in by Meiko's sense of humor and eye for adventure.

After they'd broken up, he hadn't known if he'd experience that type of attraction again.

But then he'd been gobsmacked by the sight of Garnet schussing down the hill the day he'd met her for lunch. Her mischievous smile, her drive, her love of having her fingers in everything... Damn, she made him happy. Scared, yeah. But definitely happy.

But you have to make her happy, too.

And today—he'd done the opposite.

He stood next to Zach, nursing his beer and watching Garnet dance with Cadie and Lauren. Her way of subtly dodging him, it seemed. She didn't seem angry anymore, but she did seem distant. *Be honest with yourself. That hurts more.*

"Why's Garnet on edge today?" Zach asked. "You two have a fight about balloon arrangements or something?"

"Or something," Caleb muttered.

"Ah, Christ, sorry. I was kidding." Zach took a drink from his beer bottle.

"Wish I was." Didn't seem right to spend the party in the middle of a spat, given he'd worked so hard to attend. But he didn't know what else to say, either. The next steps forward seemed too hazardous.

"What'd you do?" Zach asked.

"How'd you know it was me?"

"The same way I know it's always me with Cadie." Zach shook his head. "Didn't think the two of you would match, to be honest. But she gave me what for when I tried to tell her that."

"Yeah? How so?"

"Eh, I brought up how she hasn't stuck with anyone for a while."

He warmed at the show of loyalty, but cringed on Garnet's behalf. She'd been burned in the past. But her ex being a dick was not the same as Caleb's situation. And her inability to see that lingered in his mind, urging him to be cautious. "She's had her reasons not to commit."

Zach arched a brow. "And she's dealt with those reasons?"

He shrugged. "I can't get comfortable with her being in the backcountry. And that pushed her buttons when she picked me up from work today."

Yeah, he'd been tired at the time. But that definitely fell under the "reason, not excuse" category.

"It's a process, man." Zach gripped Caleb's shoulder. "I wasn't even in the slide, and it screwed with my head. And Cadie… We still have to work at it. Doesn't mean you can't be together while you're traveling that road, though."

"Yeah, I know." A hundred medical textbooks and journal articles on post-traumatic stress agreed with Zach. But a fist of doubt gripped his chest.

You'll let her down like you did Meiko. Learn your lesson, asshole. You've gone as far as you can—

No. Being with Garnet was worth the work to progress further. He closed his eyes, scrambling for his therapist's wisdom. *Replace the thought with a different thought.*

"I'm not done healing," he said, the words slipping out before he could stop them.

Zach's eyes lit a clear green. "Glad to hear it, buddy."

Holy awkward. His mouth dried out and he glanced away. Garnet centered a circle of her friends. Hips twitching and curls wild around her shoulders, she was like an independent light source, throwing beams of bright merriment all over the room. "I'm thinking I should be dancing with that hot redhead instead of just drooling over her."

Zach drummed his fingers on his beer bottle. "Meiko was wrong, you know."

Caleb froze. "What do you mean?"

"She didn't give you the chance to heal, was on your case way too early about getting back out there. There's nothing wrong with needing time."

And maybe that's all it would be now. Him needing more time to adapt. So if Garnet could be patient...

After clinking beer bottles with Zach, he wandered over to the pack of shimmying women and fixed a lop-sided smile on Garnet. "Can I cut in?"

After a moment's hesitation, she met his smile with a labored one of her own. "By all means."

Taking her hand, he twirled her, eliciting a squeal from her and a collection of "aw, romantic" expressions from the other women. Garnet must not have filled them in on his screw-up—they were raking him with their gazes, sure, calculating if he was good enough for their friend, but there wasn't any animosity in the evaluation.

Garnet, though, lacked her usual warmth. He tugged her into his embrace, but her grip on his shoulders was cursory at best.

Matching the beat of the music, he set them into a swaying rhythm. "How'd I get so lucky, dancing with the prettiest woman in the room?"

"Apparently, I took a liking to that charm of yours," she muttered. She lay her cheek on his chest, her actions belaying the clear "I'm seriously questioning my logic" tone underlying her voice.

A sigh shuddered through her slim frame. He settled a palm on her lower back and the other between her bare shoulder blades. Notched between taut muscles, just teasing the splashed edge of her vibrant watercolor tattoo.

Man, his hand fit well there.

She fit well against him, period.

And he needed to get his head wrapped around a way

to fit *himself* into her life without causing her angst. "I owe you a real apology."

"Yeah? For what?"

He paused. Critical to get this right. "I hit one of your buttons this morning, with being snarky about you staying safe. And I'm sorry if I was sticking my nose in where it didn't belong. But I gotta say—I was taken aback by how defensive you got."

Her eyes widened and a little wrinkle formed between her brows. "Defensive?"

"Yeah. What did you mean by being a chameleon?"

"Exactly how it sounds. I gave up things I loved and took on things I didn't, for the sake of pleasing my parents and finding a boyfriend. And I can't do that again."

"So what *can* you do, Gigi?"

She rocked back a step, dropping her arms from his neck. Even through the lowered lighting, he saw her lose a measure of the color from her cheeks.

"Garnet! Caleb!" Lachlan Reid sidled up to them. His hair looked like he'd just been up on one of the ridges in the middle of a windstorm, and a high flush rode his cheeks. Caleb would hazard a guess the guy was a few drinks in. "I wanted to say thanks again for dinner last week, buddy. That lamb was a damn masterpiece."

"You're welcome." Caleb had genuinely enjoyed getting to know the vet tech recently. But he didn't need to further their friendship at this exact minute. He wanted Garnet to answer his question.

Relief, as if she was happy for the delay, washed over Garnet's face. "Who'd you tag along with to get an invite tonight, Reid?"

"What, you getting exclusive with your parties these days?"

She rolled her eyes. "You're not staff, no matter how

much time you spend flirting with the gym manager at the juice bar."

Lachlan frowned and took a gulp from his beer bottle.

"What?" Garnet asked. Her eyes widened. "Wait. You haven't flirted with Jess in weeks. What went on with you and Marisol?"

"Nothing," the other man grumbled. "So, are you signed up for the ice-climbing session after New Year's?"

Garnet stepped closer, ringing her arm around Caleb's waist. "Totally pumped for it."

Caleb's lungs started to constrict and he breathed through it. *Be supportive.* "What'll that involve?"

Lachlan grinned at Caleb. "Glacier rescues, and for fun, climbing up Janna Falls."

Two years ago, he'd have been up there, hanging next to her. His experience of SAR had been like anyone's— periods of frustration, moments of victory, times of shattering failure. But the camaraderie… Maybe the lack of that social outlet was why he'd been feeling his isolation so clearly.

An odd emptiness hollowed around his heart, and he rubbed his chest, earning a concerned glance from Garnet.

"Sorry, muscle spasm," he lied.

She cocked a brow, but refocused on Lachlan. "Is Stella coming home for Christmas this year?"

The other man's face darkened as he shook his head. "And Maggie—that's my other sister," he added, no doubt for Caleb's benefit, "is flying off to Huatulco. I'm going to tag along to Cadie's dad's house. Apparently, he makes a beef crown roast that's, in Cadie's words, more magical than unicorn tears. Think I could trade you for one of your eggnog pies?" he asked hopefully.

"Trade me what?"

As the pair negotiated a fair exchange, Caleb rubbed his chest again. The hollow wasn't filling as fast as he'd have liked.

No way could he actually miss being out in the field. But having a purpose outside work…

There are other ways to help out.

Hell, that sounded like his mother.

And had it not been after midnight in New York, he might have dialed her up and picked her brain.

A gentle hand landed on his forearm. The stones in Garnet's rings caught the light from the fire, seemed to glow from within. Lachlan had vanished into the crowd. "Hey there, serious face. We're sure not doing a good job of enjoying this party tonight. And if anyone deserves to, it's us."

He wrapped his arms around her and began swaying to the music again. Whoever had sneaked a song onto the playlist involving some pop star whining about mistletoe deserved to be shoved out of the gondola on the way back down the mountain. "What kind of volunteer work does your search and rescue team need that doesn't involve the technical parts?"

She stiffened in his embrace. "What do you mean?"

"Exactly what I said."

"Caleb…"

He sighed. "You don't think there'd be a role for me?"

"I think if you have a hard time with me tweaking my knee while doing routine patrolling, being around real field emergencies might not be healthy for you."

His palms slipped against the silk of her dress and he dipped his head to her ear. "You know, for someone who bristled at being coddled, you sure like to throw it back my way."

"I—" She snapped her lips shut.

"You?"

"I nothing. You're right. You're the only person who knows what's right for you."

The victory of her admission fell flat. He'd been starting to hope she was right for him.

After today, he wasn't so sure.

But having the weight of her on his chest, hearing her hum distractedly with the music—he could think of worse ways to find the answer.

A few hours after stumbling the half-dozen blocks back to her place from the gondola, feet aching from her heels, Garnet woke with a start. The late night had made her overtired, both the dancing, and then putting her doubts aside to strip Caleb of his tie and shirt and sexy-as-hell pants. To lose herself under the spell of his skilled fingers and mesmerizing dirty words. But why had she woken? Nothing disturbed the room, dark in the early morning hours—

A shudder shook the bed. Her heart leaped into her throat. Caleb jolted, moaned, twisted the sheets away from her.

Jesus. He hadn't mentioned having nightmares. Should she wake him? Would he startle, or lash out?

Another shout. Then a full-on "help," but muffled, as if his lungs couldn't take in a full breath. The dim light from a crack in the blinds caught the tortured mask twisting his mouth. His arms flailed, then hugged tight to his head.

Her chest squeezed, and her eyes stung. She didn't want to scare him by shaking him awake. But she didn't want him to get into a cycle of nightmares and not get any rest.

Maybe if she called out his name, he'd wake up. She

scooted to her edge of the bed, first—he might be the kind of dreamer who woke up swinging.

"Caleb," she said firmly.

"No!" His body twitched.

"Caleb! You're dreaming. Wake up!"

A strangled scream rent the dark, the fear of death in every decibel.

Forcing words out past the terror gripping her throat, she yelled, "You're safe! Wake up!"

Cursing loudly, he jolted again. His muscles stayed stiff under the covers, plank straight except for his arms covering his eyes.

"Garnet?" he croaked, something haunted flashing across the visible part of his face.

"Hey." She crawled closer and lay a hand on his clammy shoulder. "Bad dream."

He grimaced. "Son of a bitch."

"Didn't know you had them."

He scrubbed his hands down his face. "It's been over a year."

Damn. She didn't like thinking that him working to minimize his anxiety—and her encouraging him in that—could be causing nightmares. Regret percolated in her belly.

"Come here." He held out his arms, and she snuggled into his embrace, pulling the duvet over them. One of his big doctor's hands stroked a path down her back, soothing the racing pulse thudding under her ear. The warmth of his skin soaked through her thin sleep tank.

"Shouldn't I be comforting you?" she said.

"My nightmares used to scare the hell out of Meiko." He kissed her hairline, voice shuddering across her forehead.

"I'm not one to get spooked," she promised.

Not by a nightmare, anyway. But the urge to do whatever it took to make sure he wasn't suffering? That gave her pause.

"You going to be able to get back to sleep?" he asked.

"Again, that seems like something I should be asking you."

His palm rubbed lazy circles down her spine. "You're skiing in a few hours—I don't want you to be exhausted on the hill."

"Good point. How about we both sleep in?" She walked her fingers up his chest. "Won't kill me not to get first tracks."

"It's your only day to ski off-patrol this week."

She smiled at that. "Yeah, and having a lazy morning with you sounds just as good as being first in the lift line."

Worry panged in her chest, but she shoved it to the side. She wasn't changing her plans because he told her to, or because he'd shamed her into it. She genuinely wanted to wake up in Caleb's arms, to share coffee and make waffles together.

And right now, to explore the hot gleam in his eye. He teased his fingers under the hem of her tank and played a sensuous pattern on her lower back before tucking his fingertips inside her shorts and tracing whorls on her ass.

"If we're awake anyway," she mouthed one of his hard pecs, "we might as well enjoy it. And then you might be able to fall asleep."

"Even if I can't," he said, the grin on his face erasing any visible lingering unease from his bad dream, "I'll count it a win."

Chapter Thirteen

After the sweet ministrations of Garnet's mouth, Caleb did manage to doze off. And waking up with her, her hair messy and cheek lined with pillow marks, filled him with equal amounts of satisfaction. With any other woman, he'd have felt embarrassed about his nightmare. Not with her.

Notable, and that stayed with him as the week crept closer to his holiday shifts at the hospital. What would have been a blur of snow and work crystallized into a sharp reality around Garnet. She was stealing his heart, one smile at a time. His head hit the pillow with more contentment on the nights she lay next to him.

She'd even gotten him up the mountain again—they'd had a hell of a day, racing each other down the back bowls and kissing on the rides up. And she hadn't gone on any major SAR calls, allowing him to purposefully stick his head in the sand. If he didn't acknowledge the fear that percolated in his belly every time he thought of her strapping on a harness and crampons and climbing up an icy mountain face, it wasn't there.

It wasn't there as he pushed paperwork around his desk before the clinic opened on Christmas Eve, and definitely not as he walked down the street on his lunch hour, simultaneously checking "get some fresh air" and "call Mom" off his to-do list.

"Caleb?" his mother prodded on the phone, voice

sharper than the wind blasting down Main Street. "I asked if you could send me your flight itinerary for the end of January. I'll come to the airport to pick you up."

"Aw, don't worry about it. My flight doesn't get in until midnight. I'll cab it. Or harangue a ride out of Ash." His younger brother lived in their parent's garden apartment with Caleb's nine-year-old niece.

"No way, kiddo. I want to look you in the eye and finally see for myself how you're doing. I don't care how late it is."

He should have protested the diminutive, but it wouldn't get him anywhere. His mom had always insisted there was no statute of limitations on the rights that came with giving birth. "I've kept you up to date."

Sort of.

She cleared her throat. "And most of those times, you've told the truth."

His back stiffened. "In the past month I've gone skiing, attended a party at the top of the mountain and found a girlfriend." Good thing Garnet wasn't around. They hadn't talked about labels yet. "And I tried a new kind of therapy this week—biofeedback. What more do you want from me?"

"For you to sound proud of yourself when you list those things off, not confrontational."

Why should he be proud of things that people did on a regular goddamn basis? He just wanted to be normal again.

Longing rolled through him, followed by a cold bucket full of shame. *Normal*...

What kind of doctor was he being to his patients if he didn't normalize his own anxiety? What kind of jerk was he being to *himself*?

"Confrontational is a bit harsh, Mom."

"Is it?" Her voice gentled. "Be kind to yourself, Caleb. Don't forget you don't need to be a superhero."

Okay, time to change the subject. "You must think I'm in a dire place if you're letting 'girlfriend' roll by without addressing it."

"Oh, I hadn't forgotten," she said cheerfully.

"Figured. Anyway, how's work?" He halted at a crossroad of Main Street, across from the town square. Left would take him to the village gondola. Right, past a row of shops and eventually curving to a halt at Evolve. He checked his watch. He had a half hour. Enough time to give Garnet her Christmas present—with him working the next couple days and her going to her parents' for dinner tomorrow, he wouldn't get to see her until after the holiday. A right turn, it was.

"Tell me about her," his mom said.

Obeying, Caleb filled her in on Garnet's pertinent details—name, rank and serial number stuff. He rounded the corner, and a bitter wind picked up. He pulled his beanie down and ducked his chin behind the collar of his ski jacket.

Evolve came into view. A mental picture surfaced of Garnet in leggings and an artsy tunic, hair fixed atop her head with clips and pins. Need bolted through his middle. Damn. Twenty-five minutes, and being at her workplace, wasn't going to be enough time to explore that.

"Anything else you need to know about her?" he asked, rushing up the front stairs of the facility so that he could hold the door open for one of his senior patients, a kind woman who seemed to know everything about the town. Her mischievous smile and *Golden Girls* glasses were fixtures at the grocery store, Peak Beans and the bakery. "Actually, give me a minute, Mom. Just ran into a patient." He shifted the speaker of the phone away from his mouth. "Gym day, Gertie?"

She shook her head. "Had an acupressure appointment. Dr. Martin referred me, and am I ever grateful. Garnet knows her stuff. But then, you know her quite well, don't you, dear?" Her faded green eyes twinkled.

Ah, so his relationship was making the rounds, then. He wasn't sure what to think about being bandied down the local gossip chain. He did like that he'd graduated from a formal "Dr. Matsuda" to "dear" in Gertie's book, though, so he'd take it.

"You tell me," he teased back. "I'm betting your ear is closer to the ground than mine."

She patted his arm. "Oh, likely." She leaned in, and he caught the scent of the lavender essential oil Garnet used for relaxation. "She used to come into my bakery when she was a tiny little thing. Loved my chocolate chip cookies." Her gaze fixed on a mud-splattered truck pulling into the curb. "There's my grandson. And remember, Nancy still uses my secret recipe. If you were looking to stock up on a dozen or two."

Caleb rubbed the back of his neck and nodded at Gertie's grandson, the sheriff. Garnet's SAR supervisor. His stomach lurched. Swallowing back a flood of saliva, he ducked into Evolve. "Sorry, Mom. Hellos always turn into more around here."

"Right." His mom's voice was a little raspy. "I'll be honest, honey, I didn't think you'd enjoy small-town work. But I'm impressed."

His cheeks warmed, from pride as much as from getting out of the wind. "I'm trying."

"Now, about that girlfriend…"

He snorted and hovered outside the door to the hallway where Garnet's treatment room was. "What about her?"

"Any chance you'd get her to come with you for your trip home?"

Bring Garnet across the country to meet his parents a month from now? Heat rose up his neck, and he reflexively scanned to make sure none of the handful of people in the glassed-in front atrium were listening, even though he knew full well they couldn't hear his mom through the phone. "Too soon. We're not that serious."

A squeak sounded behind him. He spun. Garnet stood, hand on the door, face pale.

His stomach hit the floor.

"Crap, gotta go, Mom." He ended the call, sending Garnet an apologetic smile. "That wasn't what it sounded like."

"No, it's fine." Her throat bobbed. She spun on a heel and headed back toward her treatment room. "You're right, we're not that serious."

He chased after her. Actually chased. Desperate? Sure. Worth it? Damn straight.

She ducked through the doorway and gripped the handle.

Heart sinking, he held a palm to the door lest she try to slam it in his face. "Garnet, that's not what I meant. My mom was prying. Asking if I was going to bring you along on my vacation home at the end of January. And though a week in New York with you sounds like fun—" more than, really "—I don't think we're quite at the parent-meeting stage yet."

Troubled gray eyes met his. "I didn't like hearing you minimize our relationship. Which is stupid, considering we haven't really defined it yet. I don't know why I'm upset." Letting go of the door handle, she wrung her fingers. "God, why am I telling you all this?"

He covered her twisting hands with both of his and

squeezed. "Because this is what people do when they're getting into each other? Feel like up is down and left is right and like the impossible might just not be that after all?"

And like it was really time to shut his trap.

She worried her lip with her teeth. "Caleb…"

"I want to call you my girlfriend, Garnet."

"Being someone's girlfriend has never gone well for me," she whispered. She backed into her treatment room, looking around wildly for a few seconds before hurrying over to a table and fussing with the tiny bottles of oil lined up in precise rows. A few toppled over and she cursed.

He went over to the counter next to her and hitched a hip onto it, rubbing her shoulder gently. "And riding chairlifts wasn't working for me, but I did it anyway."

She gripped the edge of the small table and closed her eyes. The low light from a floor lamp glinted copper in her hair. She had it pinned up like he'd pictured in his brief fantasy. And all he wanted to do was pull it down, one clip at a time.

He shifted behind her, curving his body around her softness and bending his head to kiss her temple. "It was nice to be able to use a certain G-word with my mom."

"I don't know."

Hands slackening at her sides, he took a second to breathe away the nerves that rose at her uncertainty.

"I get it," she continued. "You like the solidity of it. Tangible things. And what I do—everything I do—has some of the unknown to it."

"But I trust you," he said, stroking his hands along the thin fuzzy material covering her arms. He blinked in surprise at his own admission.

"Do you really?"

"Best as I can," he admitted.

"I want to trust you." Her voice shook, and she leaned back against his chest. Her hair tickled under his chin. "But I question my judgment."

Protectiveness rose in his gut. He didn't want her to doubt herself. And if sharing the details of what had shaken his own foundation would help her see that he indeed trusted her… His knees wobbled under the weight of his failures. Would she be as disgusted by his reactions as he was? Push him into the territory of her untrustworthy, selfish ex-boyfriends? Couldn't get more selfish than—

"I'm glad the rescuers found me first, Garnet."

She froze.

The words dripped filth into the calming, herbal-scented space. Slid down his neck like a chunk of melting snow, like the snow the avalanche had jammed under the collar of his jacket. Holy crap, had he really just admitted that to her? His stomach calcified and he backed away, ass colliding with her treatment table.

Slowly, she turned, face marked with sympathy.

Which wasn't right. He deserved horror, disgust.

He fisted a hand in his hair and slid down the table a few inches. "I should go."

"Sit." She pointed at the stool. "Please."

His knees shook, and he sat. On the floor.

She dropped to the ground next to him, legs crossed. Her hands braced on his knee, kneading the joint in a way that seemed instinctive, unconscious. "Of course you're thankful—"

"I'm not thankful, I'm glad." He pinched his nose to stop it from stinging. "There's a difference."

Her eyes were damp and her chest rose and fell a little too fast. "How?"

"Being thankful just means appreciating what happened. Being glad means being happy about it. Means wanting that outcome repeated. Means choosing my life—" a cramp seized his ribs and he choked on a breath "—over my friends' lives."

"No one wants to die, Caleb."

"And a good person wouldn't wish his friends dead." The words cutting into his throat, thin razor slits of honesty.

Her mouth twisted, and her eyes went sad at the corners. Her hands tensed on his knee, then fell away. Good. She needed to get away from him, needed to—

"No, he wouldn't," she said, throat bobbing. Her shaking hands landed on his shoulders, and she gathered his head against her chest.

Pain pierced his chest as if her words were an oscillating saw. But he appreciated her bluntness. Finally, someone with the balls to agree with him. "Exactly."

"But that's not what you're doing," she whispered.

His muscles twinged, begging for escape, but she held him too tightly to easily get away.

"Garnet…" he warned.

"Caleb, you lived through a tragedy. I've seen a lot of them. Have been on the finding end of both pink bodies and blue ones." And she was so damn glad he'd been one of the pink—alive—ones after getting caught in such a serious slide. But some of his friends hadn't been so lucky, and he'd probably never stop grieving that. "People die, and it sucks." Her throat bobbed against his temple. "But being glad you're alive doesn't mean you want your friends to be dead."

A lump filled his throat, blocking his ability to protest further. Inhaling the calming scents of the room and of Garnet's skin, he straightened, shifting their positions. Her arms comforted in the best of ways, but he was getting a neck crick. He flopped his knees to the sides and pulled her into the space. Eyeing him cautiously, she complied, settling against his chest and gripping her hands around his wrists when he circled her with his arms.

She burrowed closer. "Getting over trauma isn't logical, and you can't reason your way out of it. And it's not helping anyone for you to be caught in an anxiety spiral."

He stiffened. The handle on the cupboard forming the base of the table dug into his back. "This is about guilt, not my PTSD."

She let out a dry laugh.

And he couldn't blame her. He recognized his nonsense. But getting called on it rankled. The back of his neck burned. "Glad you find me so amusing."

"Oh, geez. I'm sorry. But Caleb—it all connects." She shifted and knelt between his legs. "This..." She touched the pads of two fingers to his temple. "This..." Her palm landed over his heart. "And this." Taking his wrist with her other hand, she placed his hand, the one still stiffened and marked by surgeries, over her own heart, nestled between her breasts. "Everything's connected."

She probably meant it on a cellular level or something like that. But as the warmth from her palm soaked through his sweater, he couldn't dispute it, reason it away as pseudoscience. And being connected to Garnet... Something about it felt so right in among all the wrongness of the limits he'd put on himself after the avalanche. He picked up her hands and kissed them in the middles, one, then the other.

"We're connected, Caleb."

His mouth turned up. No label mattered. It was her acceptance he needed, the emotional tie. "And I'm glad for that, Gigi."

"I want to be your girlfriend," she blurted. "But..."

"But it's a big step for you. I hear you." Leaning in,

he eased them into a kiss that would give him something to daydream about when he was on shift at the hospital overnight, texting her good-nights and sweet nothings. "I know we hadn't talked about exchanging presents for either holiday, but I saw something in a window the other day and couldn't resist."

A corner of her mouth rose, then fell. "I didn't get you anything—we weren't really dating yet at Hanukkah, and I figured it was too early for Christmas presents…"

He chuckled. "It's all good. I'm probably being presumptuous by getting you something, too. So as long as you aren't weirded out that I bought you jewelry, consider us even." He tugged the three-inch square box from his jacket pocket and passed it to her.

"Depends on the jewelry," she said under her breath, untying the satin bow and opening the box. White teeth nipped at a pink lip. "Oh…" The exclamation came out on a soft breath.

His pulse skipped. "'Oh,' well done, or 'oh,' you're an idiot?"

She lifted the two bangles from the tissue paper lining, and ran her finger along the embedded stones. Tiny, dark red stones studded one, and smoky quartz, the other. That one had reminded him of her eyes. Admitting that seemed too corny, though.

Her smile turned teasing. "It can't be both?"

"It's certainly both."

She shook her head. "Yeah, it is. Because you knocked it out of the park. And you're an idiot for thinking I wouldn't like them. And now I feel *really* awful for not getting you something."

"Get me a Valentine's present," he said lightly.

Her long eyelashes shuttered for a second that had his heart racing again.

You're getting ahead of yourself.

But instead of the too-fast signal he feared, a wide smile crossed her lips. "You got it."

A chime sounded from across the room and she winced. "I'm so sorry—I have an appointment in five minutes."

Five minutes… The reminder had him springing to his feet and kissing her quickly. "Damn it, so do I. I'm going to have to jog back to the clinic."

"Be well!" she called after him, as if she'd been treating him as a client.

She hadn't done anything remotely like acupressure.

And yet, as he literally ran to work, tearing into the clinic with a minute to spare, his shoulders felt buoyed by the same lightness they had when she had treated him weeks ago. And her words—*it's not helping anyone for you to be caught in an anxiety spiral*—stuck with him as he saw his afternoon patients and then went for an after-work jog. He knew what it felt like to be buried alive. And was starting to believe he deserved to dig himself out from underneath his guilt.

Garnet caught the time on the dashboard clock of her SUV. After nine—rather late to bring Caleb the Christmas-dinner leftovers she'd promised him. Between their schedules and her going to her parents' for the holiday last night, and her call today, they hadn't seen each other since he'd visited her at Evolve.

Since she'd agreed to be his girlfriend.

Unlike Caleb, who'd been happy to share the relationship with his mom over the phone, she'd been reluctant to tell her parents. They'd have been thrilled, of course. Dating a doctor fell right into their science-y ways. But she hadn't wanted to hear how her life was less in comparison. So she'd eaten ham and Brussels sprouts and two slices of pie, and had kept her mouth shut.

And now, thanks to an afternoon search and rescue call, she was walking into the hospital far later than intended to deliver Caleb his share. What should have been a simple rescue had been complicated by her and Sheriff Rafferty getting blocked by a little avalanche. They hadn't been in danger, but it had forced them to find a new trail out.

The automatic door slid open and she made her way down the quiet hallway into the emergency room. Caleb leaned on the nurses' station, chatting with the duty nurse.

"Hey," Garnet said softly.

He strode to Garnet's side, then pulled her into a small, empty staff room. Concern lined his face. "I was about to send out a search party, but then I remembered you were the search party."

The second she'd shucked her coat, he shut the door and crowded her against the wall in the best way, pressing hard muscles everywhere that mattered. "Missed you. Wanted to thank you for listening the other day."

His lips landed on her jaw, then nibbled down her neck. His fingers dug into her hips.

She melted. Damn it, why did her limbs lose the ability to hold themselves up when they came into contact with his built form?

Because he's built, idiot.

She so didn't need the snarky inner commentary. But like her tongue, her brain didn't always follow the rules. Mentally slapping away her embarrassing tendency to lose herself in her thoughts, she gripped his biceps.

Yup, built.

Goddamned delicious, in fact. Especially when all that hard muscle was covered by a butter-soft navy sweater.

And he smelled like soap and snow and man—better even than the savory scents wafting out of the bag of food she'd brought. She dropped her head back to the wall with a moan.

"Hungry?" His soft question matched the touch of his mouth to her collarbone.

"Yeah. Can't decide what smells more edible—the leftovers, or you."

"Mmm, thanks," he mumbled. "Better get some food in you. You worked two jobs today."

Taking the bag, he set it on the four-seater table and unloaded the food, scanning her with a clinical eye. "Tough rescue? Didn't expect you to work into the dark."

"Not tough. Just irritating. A slide washed out our path." He blanched. Oh, crap. She'd spoken without thinking. "Just a small one. Happened while we were a mile away."

"Just a small one," he grumbled, sounding so much like a crotchety old man that she expected him to follow it up with "fool woman" or something else equally patronizing. He sat in one of the folding chairs and crossed his arms.

"Makes sense it would trigger you," she murmured.

"I'm not triggered, Garnet. I'm just pissed off."

Legit analysis on the being pissed-off part, but she so did not buy the not-a-trigger comment. And it matched his "it's grief, not PTSD" assessment from the other day. But thought processes didn't change overnight. She knew that personally. It took years. And even if he had to manage his PTSD indefinitely, well… As long as it was something they could keep talking about, go to therapy together if necessary—that wouldn't be what kept them from being together.

He hadn't asked her to change yet. And she wanted to

believe that he wouldn't. But if he was angry... "Would you rather I not have gone?" she asked quietly.

His mouth hung in disbelief. "The last thing I want is you near an avalanche, Garnet."

"Yeah..."

"What if you weren't a mile away? What if you were caught up in it?" His eyes glinted with wetness, magnifying the anguish. He blinked rapidly, jaw tightening until the damp sheen dissipated. And she gave him that time. He had a right to it. What he'd been through... She couldn't even imagine, even with having been involved on the rescue end of a slide.

Once his face started to relax, she promised, "I'm careful, Caleb—"

He palmed his face, muffling his deep breath. "So was I. And I still got buried. And the thought of that happening to the woman I'm falling—" Coughing, he reddened and stared at his knees.

Her pulse hitched. "Falling...in love with?"

"Seems so." The word came out strangled, and a sheepish twist marred his mouth as he made eye contact. "And it's really hard to accept you being in danger all the time. I can do something about a minor knee sprain. Not so much cardiac arrest from shock. Or a broken neck. Or missing, unrecoverable."

A list of the fatal injuries from the avalanche, no doubt. Holy God. Reality speared her gut and her eyes shuttered. What a freaking close call he'd had. Buried under a slab of cement-like snow. Struggling to breathe. Only being able to listen to his heartbeat and shouts for however long it had taken to be dug out. He could have perished, and she might never have gotten the chance to meet him. To see him challenging himself, and working with patients and—

"I'm doing my fair share of falling, too," she confessed, opening her eyes to stare into his.

Cautious hope filled his expression. "Yeah?"

"Yeah."

He leaned down to kiss her, a feather-light caress at first, then deeper. Warmth flooded her core, settling between her legs and making her squirm.

But when he pulled away, his mouth bent with unhappiness, not the satisfaction of a damned good kiss. His hands clenched in his lap.

Worry unsettled her stomach. "What's wrong?"

"My mind's looping on me. Images of you in worst-case scenarios. And I can't get it to clear." Resting his elbows on his knees, he dropped his head into his hands.

She spun her chair next to his and rubbed his back. "Hey. That's nothing unusual. And I'm no stranger to therapy. I remember learning to replace—"

"I know, I know. Replace the negative thought with a positive one. But the only positive thought I can think of at the moment is you promising not to go into the back-country."

Bitter words, but not at her. At himself. She could hear how much he hated admitting that. He knew how much he was asking of her, knew it wasn't really okay to ask it at all.

"I can't do that, Caleb. I promised I wouldn't change for the sake of a relationship again."

"You've said. Not with specifics, but you've been clear."

Stilling her hand on his back, she let out a breath. "Yeah, well, it's embarrassing. It started in high school. I was desperate to be liked, to have friends, to fall in love. I listened to their kind of music, dressed how they did, registered in courses to be with my boyfriends."

"Doesn't sound unusual for a high school kid, Garnet."

"Probably not. But it was a sign I didn't like myself very much. And in college…"

He turned enough so he no longer had his back to her. "In college?"

"More of the same. But add in drinking, which I did to try to fit in. So whenever I was interested in someone, and we were out partying, I'd drink past the point of rationality. Usually managed to embarrass the hell out of myself. One night I ended up at a bar, and there was a man there who I was friends with, but also had a crush on. We'd fooled around a little, but then he had a change of heart. Wanted to try to mend things with his ex."

Caleb let out a little groan.

Heat burned up her cheeks, but it was good to continue. Good for him to know why she could only compromise so much. "And he was clear on that. He wasn't playing around with me. But I was drunk, and went on this crazy rant with him out in front of the bar about how she didn't want him and I wanted him, and that I'd done everything I could to make him want me—joining an intramural basketball team even though I hated it, pretending to like smooth jazz… He took me home. I ended up getting sick in the cab, and in the bathtub. He made sure my roommate was taking care of me."

"Gigi…" His voice was rough.

"I know. A few weeks later, I hadn't gotten over him, so I made an idiot of myself by having a sobfest out in front of another bar. Rinse and repeat. One night I fell asleep on a friend's toilet, even."

She looked at Caleb out of the corner of her eye. No judgment lined his face—impressive. "I have other examples. That's just one that sticks out."

He traced a careful thumb along her arm. "Sounds like a binge-drinking incident more than anything."

"It was all tied together. I was super socially anxious sober, and drank to relax. To be more fun."

To try to get people to like me.

"But it wasn't more fun."

"Of course not. When I got to grad school, I didn't have time to drink as much. Started dating Bryce. Who took it upon himself to make me feel like garbage every time I went up the mountain to blow off steam or picked up a patrolling shift. Ryan knew my skill set, invited me to join SAR—I said no." Shame burned her cheeks. "Bryce had been making increasingly critical comments. We'd been together for a year. And his parents came to town—trust-fund babies from Boston—and on our way to meet them at the restaurant, he told me not to mention that I was on the ski patrol. That they wouldn't understand."

He swore under his breath. "Are you kidding me?"

"Wish I was. I finally did the right thing, though. The way he worded the request—it woke me up. We stopped at a red light, and I took my purse and left the car. Went back to his apartment, packed up my toothbrush and finally put myself first for a change. I called my parents and told them I was quitting my master's program soon after.

"It took figuring out what I actually liked, filling my life with things that fulfilled me and people who I didn't feel I had to prove myself to, to be comfortable being myself. And I was lucky. Once I figured out how to like who I was, I didn't feel the need to drink to excess anymore."

He nodded seriously. "Glad to hear it. Binge drinking can be destructive."

"Yes. As was my behavior then. Hence being unwilling to give up something that's a big part of me now."

"Garnet..." He turned his right hand palm up, and

feathered the tip of a finger of his other hand along a particularly thorny scar on the inside of his first pointer knuckle. "Right here… They tried to save the mobility. Damn, I had competent surgeons. I don't think I could have done better." He snorted. "I know, it sounds over-confident."

The acknowledgment made her mouth twitch. "But you were that good, weren't you?"

"I was."

She traced her own fingers across the visible marks. "You know what it means to have to redefine yourself."

Grit filled his voice when he replied, "I might not be as far along in the process as you, but I'm not going to spend my life looking backward. I still have a job with value, a family who matters. And I'm finding my place here. Sutter Creek should remind me of everything that scares me but for some reason it feels necessary." Languid fingers stroked up and down her spine. "You feel necessary."

A gasp escaped her. "Caleb…"

Cupping the side of her head, he brought his lips to her hairline. "Hell, you have me taking steps I never would have a few months ago, professionally and personally. I've been loving going up on the mountain again. But could you be extra cautious for me? Pick the easier jobs now and again, maybe?" His cheeks went pink again. "I'm sorry I even need to ask. But I want to keep making progress. And I want to keep being with you."

"I want that, too." Caution wasn't too much to ask. Not really. "I'll do what I can."

Chapter Fourteen

"What do you mean, you aren't able to climb today?" Ryan Rafferty stalked in front of his county-issued ATV, which was serving as incident command for a midday rescue. The fuzzy collar of his sheriff's jacket flapped around his neck with every gust of wind. He jammed his gloved hands in his pockets. His scowl was as black as his hair.

"You have four climbers. You don't need me for the ropes team. Can you put me as safety officer on this one?" Garnet asked.

A climber was injured far out in the backcountry, and it was going to be a push to get everyone home before dark. Zach and his sister-in-law, Mackenzie, were particularly hoping for speed—they had Lauren and Tavish's rehearsal dinner to get to tonight. New Year's Eve, and the wedding, was tomorrow.

"Is your knee still bugging you?" Ryan asked.

"No." She'd healed just fine since tweaking it before Christmas. But taking off the bracelets Caleb had given her and putting them in her glove compartment, combined with his "Be safe" text, kept her from wanting to climb. There were enough qualified people here that she wasn't hampering the rescue effort by refusing the assignment. "Please, Ryan."

"But I want you on ropes, Garnet. Mackenzie's safety officer."

"I can switch!" Mackenzie Dawson called out from behind Garnet, her hair blowing with each frigid gust, resisting her efforts to tame them with a braid. "I'm just happy to be here and not covered with spit-up!"

"It's your first call since you had Teddy," Ryan pointed out, hands braced on his hips.

"Which was five months ago," Mackenzie said, pinning the sheriff with a pointed look. "I just finished my ropes recert. I'm beyond good to go."

A blast of wind hit Garnet's neck. The weather almost chilled her as badly as saying no to Ryan. "And I'd be more comfortable staying out of the gully."

Ryan scowled, but nodded, and began barking orders.

Two hours later, after snowmobiling as close to the incident site as they could get and skiing up a narrow skin track for the last half mile, she stood near the top of a crevasse on the backside of Sutter Mountain. She made sure the high-angle rescue crew was following all the proper procedures as they brought up the ice climber who'd experienced an anchor fail and had a potential spinal injury from the resulting fall. His buddy had climbed the face under his own steam and had been taken out to the trailhead by snowmobile, but the wind was causing problems for packing the injured climber into the stretcher. She was keeping a close eye on the speed of ascent, as she didn't want to see any more sway to her climbers or the stretcher than she was already. The last thing they needed was a rope or anchor fail of their own.

Mackenzie and Zach were on the face, along with Lachlan and his sister.

"What's your timing on the stretcher lift, Dawson?" she asked into the radio after confirming Mackenzie was listening.

"One-five minutes." A gust of wind buffeted the ridge.

A truncated cry of pain burst from the handset, making Garnet stiffen.

"Dawson? Can I have a status update?" The pause that ensued had her counting seconds, punctuated with the occasional expletive.

Zach's voice crackled on the radio after a full hundred-and-twenty count. "We have a problem, James."

Her stomach turned. Zach's call for an official assist for Mackenzie, who'd been struck by the stretcher, made it turn even more.

A torrent of profanity roared through her brain. Ryan was back at the trailhead managing the handoff of the other climber, and the other two volunteers present were certified only for the hasty alpine team. If Mackenzie's injury was serious enough, Garnet would have to join the rescue as soon as Ryan could get to the site to relieve her as safety officer. Caleb would just have to understand.

"Copy, Cardenas. To confirm, you have an injured SAR team member who requires assistance up the face?" Never the plan. Damn, damn, damn.

"Correct. Dawson came into contact with the stretcher and my initial survey indicates she's broken her arm, distal humerus. I'm working on a splint and will stay with her while Lach and Mags bring the climber up. We need another stretcher for Dawson."

"Copy, Cardenas. One more stretcher and another transport." She cleared her throat. "Sheriff Rafferty, do you copy? One more stretcher and another transport?"

Ryan confirmed his understanding, his response spitting with anger.

He was still seething hours later on the side of the snowy back road where they'd parked their vehicles.

"Had you been in the gully in the first place," he accused, "this wouldn't have happened."

Defensiveness tweaked the base of her spine, despite having played the "what if?" game for the entire schlep off the mountain. She coiled and bound one of the ropes and shook her head. "Mackenzie handled herself the same as I would have, Sheriff Rafferty. The situation wouldn't have gone any differently had she and I been in opposite roles."

He bristled. "Screw the formality, Garnet. Why the hell did you back out on me today?"

"I wasn't prepared to climb." She'd promised she'd be extra cautious, and had tried her best to follow through. And the litany of urgent text messages she'd just received from Caleb had confirmed he hadn't been prepared for her to climb, either. He was at the hospital, and had heard about Mackenzie's accident over a paramedic's radio.

"You climbed just fine when pressed into it."

"Didn't have a choice at that point," she defended. Her fingers shook and she gripped the rope until it felt like the polyester would leave marks on her palms.

"You have a choice to be a team player, or not. And if you're going to be on the ropes rescue team, I need you to be able to fill all the roles."

"Hey," she said in a low voice, her own doubts echoing his. Had she made the right call? "I'm permitted to refuse tasks that I don't feel I can safely perform. Mentally, I was better on the sidelines today. So don't spit out veiled threats. You know I put team safety first. The people who climbed today were just as well trained as I am. Does it suck Mackenzie got injured? Yes. Could it have happened to me just as easily had I been down there? Yes—"

Ryan held up a hand, his ruggedly handsome face a little gray around the edges. "Sorry. You're right." He closed his eyes for a second.

"Sorry," he repeated. "You followed procedure. And I respect that."

Nausea rose at the back of her throat, pushed up by the truth of the situation. Other than Caleb's request, she'd had no reason to back out, and someone had ended up hurt because of it. Telling Ryan her decision wasn't responsible for Mackenzie's accident was one thing. Actually believing it herself was another.

Putting the rope in the supply box, she braced a hand on the county ATV and closed her eyes. She'd done it again. Had changed herself for the sake of a relationship, and the shame of that—

Hang on. The feeling tightening her spine wasn't shame. Yeah, she was disappointed with today's outcome. It always sucked to have someone get hurt. But she'd meant what she said to Ryan. She hadn't been in the right mental space to perform the rescue. A preoccupied climber was an unsafe climber. And there was nothing wrong with making that decision. She'd spent years learning to trust her gut. And on this one, she was going to listen.

She'd been telling herself she wouldn't compromise herself again. That in order to like herself, she needed to put herself first. But unlike that time with Bryce, if she slammed the door on Caleb, it wouldn't feel freeing. She'd be letting fear control her again—the fear of losing herself this time instead of the fear of losing friends, but still fear. And what was the point of clinging to a half-developed version of the person she could be? Her life was better with love in it. And if making that love work meant give and take, then she'd find a way to do that without sacrificing everything she'd rebuilt.

Caleb stood outside Mackenzie's curtained ER cubicle and bent over to brace his hands on his knees. His breath came in rapid pants. Garnet had texted him more than once to assure him she was perfectly safe, but his rational brain refused to acknowledge reality. It was way too easy to picture her lying on the gurney instead of Zach's sister-in-law. Being hauled in on a stretcher, pale and in pain. And him racing in like Andrew Dawson had, looking like his damned world was falling apart. Thankfully for Mackenzie and Andrew, it was just a broken arm.

But the shattered devastation on Andrew's face before he'd known his wife was going to be okay—that was going to stick with Caleb for a while. *That could have been me.* His skin tingled and his vision went fuzzy on the edges, and his ribs felt like they were shrinking, caving in on his lungs…

Get a hold of yourself. Breathe. Do your job.

"Caleb?" Zach, who'd come around the corner from the waiting room, eyed him with concern. "What's up, buddy?"

"Just set Mackenzie's arm." He took in a too-shallow breath. "What are you doing here?"

Ouch. More of a snap than he'd intended. He winced in silent apology.

"Here to check on Kenz," Zach said. "I was down in the gully when she got hurt. Made things a little complicated for a bit. But your woman's one hell of a climber, Cale. She led the team like a champ."

What little blood had been left in Caleb's face trickled out, leaving his skin numbed. *Gully. Hurt. Complicated.* Zach's words pressed in from all sides, stopping any rational thought. His mouth gaped, and he couldn't close it.

Zach took him by the shoulder and squeezed. "Maybe you need a break before you move on to your next patient, eh? You look rough."

He jerked his head. "Fresh air. Five minutes."

Striding away on shaking legs, he repeated the request to the duty nurse and headed down the sterile hall and through the front doors. A frosted-over herb garden bordered the right side of the entrance, and he found a bench and sat. Christmas lights strung along the cedar hedge cast colored beams over the scrubby plants and gravel path. Rubbing his arms against the cold—his lab coat did a piss-poor job of keeping him warm—he tried to get his chest to loosen.

"Hey." Garnet's soft voice drifted over his shoulder. Gravel crunched, even steps, way slower than his racing heart. "I was coming to see if you wanted to grab dinner in the cafeteria. Saw you bolt out here."

"Yeah. Coffee break," he lied, staring straight ahead.

She sat next to him on the bench and took his bare hand in between her knitted mittens. She still had her SAR uniform on, a yellow jacket with blue lettering and black ski pants. In a past life he'd have found it a massive turn-on. He squeezed his eyes shut and rubbed a thumb along the base of her palm.

"Thanks for patching Mackenzie up," she murmured. "What a crappy day."

"Mmm." Anything more than single syllables would get stuck in his throat at this point.

"Why won't you look at me? Are you mad?"

"Nope." He gripped her hand tighter. Maybe if he held on long enough, she'd stay out of danger. Pressing his lips together, he finally looked her in the eye. Irritation flashed silver in her gray irises. "Everyone's been giving me glowing reports about how well you did, climbing down a sheer rock face to haul Mackenzie up."

And that came out as criticism instead of praise. Oops. Unintended, but by the twitch of her jaw, she'd picked up on it.

"I tried to stay on the sidelines. Really. Pissed the sherff off to no end by asking to be safety officer instead of being the litter attendant—my usual role." Brows drawing together, she dropped his hand and crossed her arms. "I normally wouldn't have held back."

"But you did because of me." His throat tightened, and he swallowed against the resistance. He wrapped an arm around her shoulders and dropped his forehead to her crown. Little curls had escaped her braid. They tickled his nose. Even after what had to have been a sweaty climb, she still smelled good. Like fresh air and hard work. "Do you want an apology or something? Because I don't know if I can give you one."

She twisted her hands in her lap, staring at her mittens. She wasn't changing because Caleb wanted her to be something different. He clearly hated asking her to compromise. If she chose to step into a different role in SAR, it would be because she wanted to. But it was hard to hold on to her earlier confidence when he was in a negative space.

So show him that there's a positive.

"I don't expect an apology," she assured him. "I—I want you to be able to move forward, to heal to the extent you're able. And not to have to rush it. I get that PTSD symptoms could be a part of your life indefinitely, and because of that, a part of mine as long as we're dating. And yeah, what I do out in the field, it matters. But I matter in other places, too. I want to matter to you."

His shoulders sagged. "You do. You're smart and skilled and passionate. I love, uh, those things about you."

"Caleb…" She loved "things about him," too. But she wasn't going to dive in to three important words until she knew he was ready to say them, too. She was, however, ready to put forward her compromise. Turning her head, she kissed his neck. "Just so you know, we don't need to hurry."

"I feel like I'm competing with the satisfaction you get when you go out in the backcountry. And I know how much of a rush that is."

"Was that why you used to volunteer?" she said. "The rush?"

"No. That's why I was involved in backcountry ski films. Couldn't beat the adrenaline of being on camera. Up until the point it almost killed me." He barked out a half laugh, half cough. "But search and rescue was about helping people. And I get you wanting that in your life. Today alone—you did impressive work."

She sat back a little and took both his hands in hers. Hopefully her wool mittens would take away some of the December sting—he was not dressed for the elements. "Thanks. Poor Mackenzie, though. It was her first call since having her baby. Did you see Andrew? He was probably climbing the walls—"

"Garnet," he interrupted. "I can't handle that being me. Getting notified to come in here because you…" His eyes shuttered. "Or being on shift when…" Another long pause, as if he couldn't find any words that quite fit. "When I heard the radio call, that you were the lead rescuer, I couldn't breathe. It was like being under the snow all over again. I don't want to have the phone ring like it did for my parents, to be informed you were buried in an avalanche field. Except unlike that call, you didn't make it. I can't do that."

"I hear that." But *she* could do something. And she was still prioritizing herself. For once, she'd invest in a relationship on equal terms. Warmth spread through her, despite the wind slapping icy stripes on her cheeks. "I'm not going to ask that of you."

His shoulders sagged. "I know. I figured we'd get to this point."

"Hey." She caught under his chin with her finger and tilted it up, kissing him softly. "Not what I meant."

"Huh?"

"What's the point of being myself if I'm still being controlled by fear?"

He pressed his fingers between his eyes. "I don't follow."

"I've been so worried about keeping what I have that I didn't think about the fact that something new could be better."

A few flakes of snow landed in his dark hair as he slowly shook his head. Taking her hands again, he squeezed. "What exactly do you mean?"

"I can step back from the ropes team," she said, the plan she'd cobbled together on the drive home spilling out in a rush. "Work the hasty alpine team, maybe, or go get my trainer's cert and try the classroom out. For a season. Then we can reassess."

"But…" His hands grew slack. "I won't be the jerk who asks you to give up something you love, Garnet."

He…he wouldn't? But… No. He wasn't supposed to say no. Her heart twirled to the cold cement, like the flakes swirling around them. Not a thunk. Just drifting down, making her slowly feel the pain of having put herself out in a major way, and him refusing it. Tears stung her eyes. "You *are* asking me to give up something I love. *You.*"

He rubbed his throat. "Better than your self-respect."

She shot to her feet, clenching her hands. No damned way did he get to tell her that compromising would mean losing her self-respect. It wouldn't. She was offering this because it felt right, not because he'd made her feel she was less to be on SAR, like Bryce had done. So why the hell was he resisting? Unless… "I assure you, I can have both. You can, too. But you're running from taking chances. Letting it stop you from enjoying your life the way you deserve to… From loving me."

Her words hung between them.

He didn't correct her.

Pain sliced through her chest. She didn't have firsthand experience watching him wield a scalpel, but he certainly used silence like a knife.

"Nothing? I spill my guts, and I get *nothing*?" she said, hearing the shrillness in her voice. God. Who cared about her tone? He deserved every ounce of her ire.

"Garnet," he rasped. "You're *everything*. But I got stuck under a river of snow, and it changed me. Which I've learned is okay. I don't do the same job, but I'm still making a difference in people's lives. And my goalposts for what it means to be healthy are different, and they shift sometimes, but I'm happy with where I'm aiming these days. For me, adjusting to my new reality, it's about doing a little better every day. But for you…changing like this would be the opposite. It would be less."

Not something he got to decide. "I'm telling you it wouldn't be."

"You said you weren't going to change your mind."

Her mouth gaped. "Did you not want me to? Was it going to be safer for you if I didn't? If there was always going to be an endpoint?"

"No—"

"Oh, my God." She backed away a step. "So much for 'buy me a Valentine's present.' You didn't think this could last. 'You're everything.' Yeah, right."

"Garnet—"

"Don't. I can't be perfect, and I don't expect perfection

from you—" Unable to stop tears from dripping down her cheeks, she wiped them away, the wool of her mitts scratching her cheeks. *Get a hold of yourself. You deserve better than this.* "But I can't be with someone who isn't willing to fight to be with me just as hard as I had to fight to figure out who I am."

Caleb shook his head. "Fighting's not the right word for how I need to live my life. I need to be persistent, sure. But my mental health isn't about a battle. It's about stepping stones."

She clenched her hands into fists. "Let me step with you, then."

"I can't—" His voice cracked. "I can't hold you back like that."

"Stop pretending to be noble. This isn't about me. This is about you being afraid."

He let out a sad laugh. "Gigi—"

"So this is it?" she cut in.

"I don't see how it can be any other way."

"Yeah, that's crap. You can see other ways. You're just not willing to try them." Oh, Jesus. How was she supposed to be his date at the wedding tomorrow? She glared at him. "I know you wanted to come to the wedding tomorrow, want to fit in—I can't go with you. Stay home. Don't. Whatever. Just stay away from me."

And before he could respond with something to temper her anger over his unwillingness to risk his heart, she spun on a heel and left.

Chapter Fifteen

Around noon on New Year's Eve, Caleb paced his kitchen. Damn it. Garnet had dragged more than just his heart with her when she'd left the hospital's herb garden last night; she'd taken his chance to be a part of the town, too. Should he go to the wedding, or not? Turning down the invitation seemed rude. But showing up seemed like directly going against her wishes. She hadn't meant one letter of her *whatever*. She wanted him to stay far away. And would anyone even want him there, once they found out how he'd let her down?

I won't be the jerk who asks you to give up something you love.

She should have called him a liar after he'd said that, not after saying she was everything.

She was everything to him.

And that was the problem. He couldn't bear to lose everything—not again. The avalanche had ripped through his life, churned it up just as it had the mountain slope. Garnet would grow to resent him. Just like Meiko had, another slow deterioration into dislike and frustration.

Or worse, not to have it deteriorate. To be disgustingly, exceedingly happy. And then to have the sheriff knock on his door…

Voicing something far cruder than *damn it*, he flipped his laptop open and pressed the button to call home before the sun went down on the East Coast—his Friday habit, lately.

No, not home. This is home.

Or it should have been, had he been willing to risk enough to stick. But he hadn't, and he wouldn't, and now he'd have to live with being an outsider...

The Skype screen flickered to life and a pair of brown eyes peered at him from behind a pair of black-rimmed glasses similar to his own. Not the eyes and glasses he'd expected, though. He arched a brow at his brother. "Why are you on Mom's computer?"

"Installing some things for her," Asher said, hands braced on the back of his head. Hair wild, beard overlong, T-shirt looking like it was going to split on his biceps— his brother had been spending too much time at the gym and not enough in the barber's chair. Caleb matched him in six-plus-feet height, but lacked the linebacker build. "Quite the Eeyore cloud over your head, big brother."

Caleb ignored the jab. "Let your hair get any longer and you'll look like a *Game of Thrones* extra."

His brother flipped him the bird. "What was with the stuffed trout you sent Ruth? Weirdest Hanukkah present I ever saw."

"I was telling her about catching one off my dock and she wants me to teach her how to fly-fish when you're here in the summer. I picked that out to tide her over."

"Well, she loved it," Asher said gruffly.

She's had too little to love lately went unsaid. Caleb knew it had been indescribably rough on his brother and niece since Asher was widowed. "Is she around? I need an update on her titanosaur project. I've been promised a trip to the museum when I visit." His nine-year-old niece regularly whupped his ass in head-to-head fact battles. Made sense—if anyone was going to have a mind for trivia and asking questions, it was the daughter of a librarian and a science teacher.

If I had a daughter with Garnet, she'd be like Ruth. Whoa.

Slow down, champ. He needed to get over Garnet, find someone more low-key.

The hairs on the back of his neck tingled. Low-key didn't mean danger-free. There were car accidents, random violence, cancer… Damn, how had Asher managed his grief this past year? Losing his husband *and* worrying about Ruth?

But no way is anyone going to make you smile like Garnet does. Low-key doesn't matter for crap in the face of her smile…

"Hey! Wake up!" Asher clapped his hands in front of the screen.

"What?"

"I was trying to tell you that Ruth's at the deli with Mom, but you spaced out on me. Geez. Why do you look so tired?"

"I've been working nights lately."

"Nah, it's not that," Asher said. "It's like you're soul tired."

Jamming his fingers in his hair, he closed his eyes. A twinge reverberated up the tendons in his right hand— the joints were stiff this morning, probably from his extra shifts this week and sitting out in the cold yesterday. "I'm fine."

"Mom made it sound like you've been loving life in Montana." Asher took a sip from a coffee mug. "But you don't look like a guy who's loving anything."

"You'd be wrong there."

"Really? Things getting serious with this woman of yours?"

"Things *were* getting serious."

His brother's belabored sigh almost came through the computer screen. "And here you had Mom convinced it was meant to be."

Caleb shook his head. It was too much of a stretch to believe Garnet was meant for him. Love shouldn't require giving up an important part of your life for the other person. Or living in fear every day. *You're already doing that—how would it be any different?*

"Garnet and I weren't going to last." Caleb's voice cracked and he cringed.

"She drew a hard line with you?"

"No." His stomach turned. Garnet had done the opposite, and her willingness to sacrifice had made him feel less worthy of anything he'd ever been offered in his life.

But pushing forward, damn the consequences... He tried to envision walking up to her. Apologizing. And then getting a phone call three months, three years, three decades from now that she'd been in an accident, and hadn't been as lucky as he had. Acid burned the back of his throat.

"It's you, then," Asher said.

"Why do you say that?"

"The Eeyore cloud, jackass. I know it well."

Caleb's cheeks heated. "Good to know I'm that transparent."

"You have the option to be with the person you love, and you're not doing it because...why?"

He fed his brother a few lines about resentment and Garnet's offered compromise.

Asher let out a low noise. "She must really love your sorry ass."

"And I love her, so how can I accept that?"

Asher lifted a shoulder. "People give things up for the

bigger picture. Hell, Alex moved across the country for me. And once we decided to become parents, I changed jobs—"

"And he *died*."

"I'm aware." Asher laughed, a harsh, rough sound.

Caleb drummed his fingers on his desk. "Don't take this as criticism—it's not—but how the hell can you laugh? Between the avalanche and now, I only managed to start a few weeks ago."

"Because of Garnet?"

His brother spoke the truth he wouldn't let his mind dwell on. "Yeah."

"For God's sake, Cale."

"Yeah," he repeated.

"I laugh because I have to. Otherwise I'd be a crap dad. And Ruth needs me more than my sorrow does." Asher leaned back in his seat. "Do you know what I would do to get time back with Alex?"

A "Considering how much I would do to not get caught in that avalanche? Probably a ton" response was on his tongue, but he held it in. No. The slide had been horrific for sure, and for the families who had lost loved ones it had been life-altering in the worst of ways. But for Caleb personally, it wasn't comparable to terminal cancer. Enough good had come out of the avalanche. Probably added ten years to his life, given the stressful rat race that was surgery. And a new hometown, and people he loved…

Not the one you most want to love.

"You don't regret it? Given the pain you've gone through?" Caleb said.

A profane vow filled the air. "Never. Not for a second."

His gut hollowed and he stared into Asher's serious face.

"What's the next step, then?" his brother continued.

"I don't know." Skiing down a mountain was one thing.

Losing his love, or knowing she could lose him… An entirely different stratosphere. "I'm scared."

"Good. That means you're alive. Be glad about that."

Caleb snorted.

"What?"

"Not long ago, someone smarter than me told me it's okay to be glad to be alive."

Asher pushed his glasses up with a single finger. "If you hadn't figured that out on your own, most of the human race is smarter than you."

"Yeah, yeah."

"Picture her with cancer."

Caleb froze in his chair. His stomach clenched. "Where did that come from?"

"Do it." Asher tented his fingers and waited, staring unflinchingly.

Closing his eyes, Caleb tried to envision Garnet lying in a hospital bed, bald from chemo like Alex had been… Nausea licked the back of his throat, and he squeezed his eyes tighter to hold off the moisture threatening to gather. "Damn, Ash…"

"I know. But when you picture that, where do you picture yourself?"

"At her bedside." Caleb blinked, stared down at his lap. "Holding her hand."

"Liar. You'd be arguing with her oncologist about something."

A single "*Ha*" escaped his throat. "And holding her hand."

"Okay, well, bad example. Cancer's not going to scare you off. A car accident, then. She's getting pulled out. And you are…"

He didn't answer, just put a fist to his mouth. The insides of his nostrils stung. If he cried in front of Asher, he'd never live it down—

"With her. Right," Asher said, sobering further. "And if she was two feet under a snow sheet? With a broken leg and a wrecked hand—?"

"Asher."

"Where would you want to be, Caleb?" The biting tone left no room for anything but honesty.

"Under the snow with her. Holding her. Telling her there would be enough air and she'd see colors other than blue again, and—" His voice broke. Damn it. Palming his face, he breathed deeply.

"So, tell her that. That you're scared as hell of losing her but you want to be with her, anyway."

"You're right."

"I know I am." Smugness rode the words. "Go tell her you were wrong."

Garnet stepped into the commons of the Episcopalian church around the corner from Evolve and took a deep breath. Arrangements of deep purple lilies and white snowdrops bracketed the entrance into the sanctuary, and a handful of other bouquets dotted the altar, but other than that, decorations were sparse. The fault of the location change, most likely. It was howling like a banshee outside—not exactly the weather for a ceremony on Lauren and Tavish's back deck, like they'd planned for.

Gah, just being at a wedding was torturous today. For five years, not being married hadn't fazed Garnet. Every day she'd spent learning how to help people heal or out patrolling had been one she hadn't been shacked up with Bryce and stuck titrating chemicals in a university lab. But falling in love with Caleb had thrown her.

She'd gotten used to it.

To waking up with his hard pecs at her back, and sharing cold pie for breakfast before dragging him up for first tracks. As she stared at the feet of the trio preparing to play, her mind drifted. Many more indulgent mornings of pastries and making love and she might start dreaming of pledging to cherish a certain stubborn, handsome doctor.

But if he's going to dictate my feelings to me, why the hell would I want that?

She was three seconds away from the pinch in her nostrils turning into full-fledged tears. At least she had an excuse—no one was going to question damp eyes at a wedding. But just in case she needed an escape route, she slid into a pew at the back and buried her nose in the program.

The strains of a cello filtered through her unease. Turning to face the rear doors of the sanctuary, she tried to swallow down the lump in her throat. Someone shuffled into the pew, taking the seat beside her. She was about to turn and say hello to whoever it was, but a familiar throat cleared. The hairs on the back of her neck prickled. She kept her attention on the back door. What the hell was he doing, sitting next to her? Anger simmered through her limbs.

"Hey," he said. A low, devastating greeting.

The tears she'd been trying to hold back sprang forward.

She gritted her teeth. Only the bride and groom deserved her tears today. Happy ones. Not hot, needling ones like the ones trickling down her cheeks.

Shaking her head to signal she wasn't in the mood to talk and didn't have any plans to face him, she dabbed at her tears with a Kleenex and hugged her arms across her chest.

"You look amazing," he murmured from behind her. "Teal is your color."

"I know." She'd been looking forward to showing off the long-sleeved knit dress for him. It was super simple, but smoking hot. "But p.s.—we're not talking right now."

"Garnet…"

"No."

"But—"

She cut off his protest with a raised hand as Lauren's older brother, Andrew, appeared in the doorway, part-nerless. Poor Mackenzie—her accident yesterday had meant she was too injured to be a bridesmaid. She was ensconced in the front row, cast on her arm and no doubt hopped up on painkillers.

Garnet could use a few of those. Dull the edges of yesterday's emotional cuts.

The music began, the rounded, emotional notes filling the space to the exposed rafters. And the shattered fragments of her heart that were left in her chest swelled, too. Against all odds, a gooey, warm-like-a-fresh-baked-cookie sweetness spread through her chest.

Garnet cracked a smile. Yeah, it trembled on the edges. But she wasn't going to let Caleb's shortsightedness or the electric buzz running along her back from having him in such close proximity ruin what was supposed to be a great day.

Cadie and Zach paused before entering the sanctuary as the honor attendants, their son between them wearing a tiny tux and holding a ring bearer's pillow. Cadie's dress was long, a deep plum color, and she wore a pretty faux-fur-trimmed capelet that Garnet immediately coveted.

Lucky bastard, she mouthed at Zach as he came even with her row.

Her boss winked and mouthed back, *You know it.*

A pair of tears trailed down her cheeks. Good grief. The bride and groom hadn't even come into view yet. She tugged another tissue out of her purse and wiped away the evidence.

Caleb bent to her ear. "Saw that."

"Sue me," she muttered.

The song changed to a cello solo, and Lauren and Tavish appeared in the doorway, hands joined. A simple white dress floated around Lauren's pregnant belly, classic and gorgeous. And the how-the-hell-did-I-get-so-lucky awe on Tavish's face made it obvious he treasured his bride.

"That's nice," Caleb whispered. "Two people walking toward their future, hand in hand."

"Are you kidding me right now?" She turned her head slightly so he'd hear her barely-louder-than-a-breath question, and caught her first glimpse of him. Mouthwatering three-piece charcoal suit. Hair a tad messy, but purposeful. Those infernally sexy, thick-rimmed glasses. And a look of exhaustion that suggested he'd slept no better than she had. She gritted her teeth, refusing to feel sorry for him.

He shifted closer, breath tickling the back of her ear. "I'm not kidding in the slightest." His voice was as rough as the snow in the back bowl by the end of the day.

"You're really crappy at not talking."

"I'm really crappy at a lot of things. And I'm sorry I let you down." His hands settled on her hips.

Have you no shame? Pull away.

But… It was the processional. Yeah, the fuss of a big wedding wasn't her style, but she was still a sucker for a white dress and swelling music. It got her every freaking time. And his muscular chest made for an excellent backrest. Physical, and emotional.

A fraction of a sniffle behind her, just audible over the

music, caught her ear. She glanced back at Caleb, who sent her a sheepish smile. *Don't fall for those reddening eyes, James. Give him a tissue, sure, but no more of your consideration.*

But as love-filled vows were exchanged, Garnet noticed full-on tears glistening on his lashes before he swiped them away with the back of his hand.

"Weddings are my Kryptonite," he said, cheeks turning as red as the whites of his eyes. "So are you, Garnet. Hear me out after the ceremony?"

Her resolve, the need to hang on to her anger, softened. Not entirely. But a few of her shards dulled. "Okay."

She stepped away from him as the ceremony started. And oh, the ceremony… Perfect words. Damn it, she deserved words that perfect, too. But also, she deserved the follow-through.

She'd let him say what he wanted to say, and maybe, just maybe, he'd come through with actions, too.

After the recessional, Garnet shrugged into her coat and gloves, intending to suggest they talk somewhere else, but Caleb cupped her elbow and tugged her into an empty corner of the church commons. Garnet felt conspicuous for all of three seconds, until she realized the rest of the guests were congregating around the other side of the entryway, waiting for the receiving line. Wind battered the stained-glass window behind Garnet's head.

"Quite the weather we're having," she said.

He cocked a brow. "Small talk, Gigi?"

She fisted her hands around the strap of her purse. "Don't call me that."

His face fell. "Please, will you listen?"

Fighting off another spurt of tears by pressing her lips into a thin line, she nodded. Damn, he looked handsome today. He needed a haircut in the best of ways, and an overwhelming urge to drive her fingers into those dark brown waves tingled down her arms. But if she had her hands in his hair, she'd have to kiss him...

He took one of her hands, flipped it and bent it upward, exposing a sliver of skin between her thin, stretchy gloves and her coat. A group of people left the church, and chilly air ripped through the room, nipping at the inside of her wrist. And then his lips did. His eyes closed for a second, almost reverent in the way his lids shuttered.

"Caleb." A plea, really.

"I want to be able to choose you, and have that be fair for both of us."

Her heart panged, and she squeezed his fingers. "I tried to do that, offering what I did. And you didn't trust me. I can handle you needing to go slow, or being afraid. I was honestly ready to change my life for you. And I was happy with that choice. A compromise with you wouldn't have been because you didn't accept me, or because I wasn't confident enough to be myself. It would have been because I felt like a better version of myself with you. And because I thought you'd keep trying to get okay with me climbing. But you dumped me anyway."

"I know." His mouth turned up, the curve punctuating his sadness. "But I was wrong. You're not easy to quit."

Oh, my God. How could he go around just saying stuff like that when he'd been the one to give up? No, it wasn't effing easy. She released a slow breath. "A few days ago, I'd have said, 'So don't.' Now? I have no idea."

"Can't blame you there." He shuffled his feet, his dress shoes rasping on the utilitarian carpet that lined the hallway. Stepping closer, he ran a hand down her arm, leaving behind an ache to step forward and bury her face in his solid strength. "Some hurdles take longer to jump over than others. And you tried to remove one entirely by offering to quit the ropes team, and Gigi, I love you for that—" he rubbed a hand over his mouth "—and for so many things. Everything. But you need someone who's brave enough to love you like you love everyone in your life."

Well, there went the rest of her heart. He'd wrenched it clear from her chest, held it in his capable doctor's hands. She rubbed her breastbone—how it wasn't literally flayed open, who knew—and sniffled. "And that's not you?"

Desperation strained the corners of his eyes. "I want it to be. I'm going to have to figure out how to do it, but—"

"What changed?"

"I talked to my brother, who pointed out a few things…"

She shook her head. "One conversation and you're a different man? Excuse me if I have a hard time with that."

His shoulders slumped. "I know. But Asher's a widower. He knew what questions to ask, to help me see I'm ready to fully invest. To risk losing you in order to be with you."

"Oh…" She didn't know what to say to that. "I—uh—I want to believe you. But what if this is one more situation where I'm desperately scrambling to make something work that is no good for me?"

"I get that. Let me prove it to you," he croaked, hooking one of her pinky fingers with his. Even that small contact was enough to pull her in.

She shouldn't. She should really keep her distance, stay out of his orbit. Fisting the lapels of his coat, she inhaled his comforting scent.

Wrapping his arms around her, he glanced to the side for a second, then fixed his gaze on her. The passion of his intent made it hard to distinguish his dark irises from his pupils. He spun her around, backed her against the

window and kissed her. Impatient lips coaxed a moan
from her throat.

"Caleb!" *Oh, my God.* There was no way the fifty-odd
people milling around the bride and groom were ignoring them now. But how much did she care? Around zero
point two percent. His hips pressed into hers and she was
tasting the wintermint gum he must have chewed not too
long ago. "Everyone's watching."

"True." Still, he didn't pull away. His kiss turned
slower, sensual, shaking her world and her common sense.

She drew her lips from his. "That is *not* the kind of
proof I was thinking of."

She already knew they were good at that. It was the
rest of life that gave her pause.

He smiled sheepishly. "We have a few hours to kill
before the reception. Want to go for a drive?"

"In this weather?"

"We can walk to your place, then. Or go grab a coffee."

"We haven't fixed this," she bit out. "You tried to dictate what I should do, which is no better than—"

"Garnet!" Ryan Rafferty's voice had her springing
away from Caleb. The sheriff jogged across the room, cell
pressed to his ear. "How quickly can you get changed? A
car went over the embankment by RG Ranch and is half-
submerged in the river. Fire department needs help with
a midangle extraction."

"Oh, crap. I have clothes in the storage room at the station." She turned to Caleb. "Are you going to be okay?"

"Yes."

"Garnet!" Ryan barked, waving his hand. "I'm not
asking anyone in the wedding party to leave, so it's us
and Lachlan. He's meeting us at the station. Let's go!"

Caleb paled a little. He clenched and unclenched his
fists in a rhythmic fashion. Then he nodded abruptly,

caught her chin with one hand and dropped a brief, soft kiss on her lips. "Going to the EMS building, right?"

"Yeah."

"I'll give you a ride."

Chapter Sixteen

Soon after dropping Garnet at the station, Caleb got a call from the hospital. With the weather beyond terrible, air evac flights were grounded, and road conditions meant the accident victims were coming to the Sutter Creek ER instead of being taken by ambulance to Bozeman. He got in his car, recognizing the irony of having to drive in inclement conditions in order to save the life of someone hurt because of driving in the same weather.

Wind battered his car, the gusts carrying a load of snow with them. He clenched his hands around the steering wheel. No one should be out on the roads in this weather, really.

The roads Garnet is on.

Rather, the embankment she was climbing up.

Fear teased his throat, but he'd spent too much time in therapy—and, more recently, hooked up to cords and sensors at a biofeedback session—to allow the sensation to take over. He had the tools to manage this. Time to check in with his heart rate and other nervous responses, and to take control of his thoughts.

Garnet is capable. Safety is her priority.

He ran himself through a grounding exercise. It felt a little juvenile, but if keeping his eyes focused on his surroundings and reciting all the animals he could think of would stop him from shaking so badly he drove off the road, then...

Lion.
Tiger.
Dog.
Cat.

He listed a zoo's menagerie until he got to *unicorn.* Yup, ready to teach preschool. But it worked. His pulse decelerated. His breathing regulated—

He would be able to do this on an ongoing basis. Proving it to Garnet seemed the larger task.

He checked in with the doctor on shift in the ER and went to the staff room to change into scrubs in case he was needed to assist in surgery. After texting Zach to pass along that he'd be late to the reception, he waited.

Thirty minutes passed, and he grew more antsy as the seconds ticked by. Three people were trapped in the car—a twelve-year-old kid and his mother and grandmother. Hell of a New Year's Eve for that family. And as much as being at the wedding reception would have been more enjoyable, he'd do what he could to make sure the family got good news.

The back-entrance doors swung open, and a flurry of activity descended on the room. The paramedics were performing CPR on the older woman. Scratch that—a paramedic and Garnet. She was ventilating the patient, her face screwed into a look of determination.

That look smacked him right in the chest, like the jolt from the defibrillator paddles a nurse was preparing for use.

Holy crap, Garnet was meant to do this. She had the skill and the empathy to be excellent at rescue work. And no way was he going to get in the way of that.

He moved to assist with the patient, and something else hit him just as hard—her work wasn't going to get in the way of them, either. He would keep learning how to better manage his fear. Yeah, there would always be some risk. But she was careful, and sometimes, doing remarkable things required taking chances. She'd support him, he knew that. And he'd prove he trusted her. Would take the mental steps to manage his job and her job and loving her as much as he was capable of. Which right now was a whole hell of a lot. Working as a team with her and the paramedics, seeing strain and hope and, finally, relief cross her face when they got a pulse, made the medical rarity seem that much more miraculous.

She caught his eye and they moved to help unload the stretcher and rush the injured woman in for treatment.

Caleb's heart swelled. "I love you!" he called over his shoulder, jogging beside the gurney. "I might be a while."

"Want me to wait for you?" she called back.

He got sucked into triage, didn't get the chance to reply. But once he was done, he'd correct her. She didn't have to wait for him. Not this afternoon, and not in the long term. So long as she was interested, they'd be able to move forward together.

Garnet fiddled with the zipper on her thermal shirt, the aches from a hard rescue throbbing along the backs of her arms and legs. The hospital waiting-room chairs weren't helping. It was after nine—she and Caleb had long missed dinner at the reception—and other than a couple of occupied beds, it was just her and the two night nurses waiting for the team in the OR to finish up with the grandmother Garnet helped extract from the accident scene. The kid and his mom were in stable condition, but it had taken longer to get the grandmother out and shock had been an issue. A nasty accident. Garnet expected to see crunched metal and fractured trees in her sleep for a while. Some scenes stuck with a person more than others, and something about hearing "Mommy! Nana!" wrenched from a kid's throat imprinted on the brain.

She should really go home, text Caleb to meet her at the reception for drinks and dancing. But she couldn't do it. Some illogical part of her clamored to stay. As if her presence could somehow change the outcome.

For Caleb's patient, yeah.

But also for her and Caleb.

He'd trusted her today. And that mattered. She wasn't satisfied with being a solo creature anymore. She couldn't shed her feelings for him. Her whole philosophy was to be true to herself, and being miserable by being apart from him was not filling that promise.

And she needed to know the context of that *I love you*. His actions today—kissing the stuffing out of her in sight of God and all of the wedding guests, asking for the chance to prove himself, driving her to the station… Her heart clamored to hope for the best.

She didn't have to wait much longer. At a quarter to ten, quiet footsteps broke through the buzzing of the vending machine in the corner of the room and the faint beeps coming from the nurses' station.

Caleb was a sight for sore eyes. A white T-shirt stretched across his chest, and blue scrub pants rode low on his hips in a rather delightful fashion. His face was delightful, too, even though weary lines etched his eyes and a red stripe marked his forehead—probably from his surgical cap or mask or something. She still wore long johns, and what had been a careful, wedding-appropriate up-do now resembled a bird's nest. Maybe he'd find her disarray equally charming.

He stared at her as if searching for some sort of answer, and rubbed his hands over his face. "You waited."

She paused, unable to decipher his tone. "Um—" All

he possible things she could say ran through her brain.
Wanting to know if the patient was okay. Wanting to support Caleb in the case of a bad outcome or celebrate if it
was a good one. But all she could get out was "I offered
to. I thought—I mean, we got interrupted, and…" Her
voice shook, pathetic and small.

He immediately closed the last few yards that separated
them, sat sideways on the chair next to hers and cupped
her cheek. "No, Sharky. I'm just surprised."

Between the warmth of his skin and the low, steady
timbre of his admission, she downright melted. He rubbed
a circle on her cheek that was liable to put her to sleep sit-
ing up, were it not also stoking a fire deep in her belly.

*Sleep. Yeah. When I go to sleep tonight, I want to have
him next to me.* Wrapped around her, to be more specific.
Would he be ready for that again? She gazed deep into
his eyes and took his scarred hand in both of hers. The
muscles felt knotted in places, and she started to press
and massage, working out the kinks. He didn't resist the
therapy.

"How'd it go in there?" she asked.

His smile delivered enough relief that he didn't need to
follow it up with an answer. But thankfully for her curiosity, he was in a chatty mood. "We had to get a bit creative given we're not set up for major trauma surgery and
I wasn't able to do more than assist, but with that level
of shock, we had to act fast. Between Frank, Bev and
me, we made do. I was able to direct Bev in addressing
a considerable amount of the damage. The patient will
have to follow up with the orthopedic surgeon, but for
now, she's stable. Minus a spleen and full of staples and
stitches, mind you."

"Better than the alternative," she murmured.

Thumb stilling on her cheek, he nodded.

"And how are *you* doing?"

"I'm a few minutes from falling over. Adrenaline'll wear off soon."

"Right." She could feel that in the hand she held. The muscles in his fingers were twitching. "Want to hit up the reception?"

He groaned. "Can we table that for a few minutes? I just want to hold you."

"Oh…"

"Come here, Garnet." He opened his arms. "Please."

She blinked. Her insides shook. "You're sure?"

"That I want to hold you? So damn sure."

She wasn't about to protest. Her body longed for his strength, for his muscles to take on her weight.

Scooting closer, she draped her legs over his lap and wrapped her arms around his waist. The side of her face reacquainted itself with his broad shoulder. *Yeah, that's better. Much.* Between his scrub pants and her leggings, there wasn't much fabric between them, and the warmth of his thighs seeped through to the backs of her legs.

"I missed this," she said. More than she wanted to admit. "It was only a day, but I missed it. But I don't want to rush things."

He groaned and his arms tightened their embrace. One palm settled on the back of her head and the other on her lower spine. Had she ever felt this physically secure? Probably not.

Emotionally, though, she was shaking like a leaf.

His fingers tensed on her head and back. Ten separate points pressed into her skin. Ten reminders he wasn't ready? He coughed. "Today was a good test. Did I worry about you? Sure. But I wasn't paralyzed by fear. I worked through it."

"Wow. That must have been some talk with your brother."

He nodded. "Nothing like visualizing the woman you love fighting cancer, dying in a car accident and buried in an avalanche to make you realize you want to be with her no matter what."

"Buried in an avalanche?" she squeaked.

"My brother is creative," he said dryly.

The line on his forehead was fading, and she smoothed a thumb along the lingering pink. Orthopedic shoes squeaked on the linoleum. Jacy, one of the night nurses, failed to convincingly pretend to be consumed by paperwork.

"Jacy's listening," she murmured.

"Oh, no doubt." The corner of his lips quirked. "Want to go elsewhere, or are you going to make her night that much more interesting?"

"Column B." She was too comfortable, wrapped up in Caleb, to think of moving. "You know, there's a difference between changing yourself for the person you love and being inspired to be a better person within a couple. And for a while, I was so afraid of the former that I wasn't willing to see the latter. And then when I decided I could step back from SAR, and you threw that sacrifice in my face..."

"That hurt. I know. And I'm sorry." Sincerity threaded his tone. "I'm still not going to ask you to make that sacrifice for me. I truly believe I can learn to be okay with you going into the backcountry."

"Caleb." She guided his gaze back to hers with a palm to his jaw. "If my climbing is a trigger for you, it's not fair that you have to live with that every day. There are other ways I can help the SAR crew, behind-the-scenes stuff."

"I know. I've considered volunteering to do some of

that myself, if I feel up for it. But you—you're magnificent, Garnet. You need to be in the field."

They untangled a bit. His grip loosened, and she shifted backward a few inches.

"God, for all I was getting after you for not letting me make decisions for myself—I'm having a hard time trusting that my fieldwork is the best for you," she admitted.

His smile turned wry. "Just like there's nothing wrong with compromise in a relationship, there's nothing wrong with the people you love forming part of your motivation to better ourselves. To be healthier." He kissed her, lingering and sweet, his lips playing over hers with masterful skill. Enough to make her squirm. Her legs moved restlessly over his lap.

A flare of heat brought out the rich brown in his irises and he splayed a hand across her knees to still the edginess. "We really should have gone elsewhere. Say, to my house. My bed."

A squeak came from the nursing station, and Garnet laughed and stood, pulling him out into the empty hall. The beam of light from the brightly lit emergency room cast long shadows down the after-hours-darkened corridor. "We've already been a spectacle today. Time for privacy."

Like that earlier spectacle at the church, he pinned her against the wall. But this time, no one was looking. Just her and him, and a thin layer of clothing separating their needy bodies.

And nothing separating their hearts.

He nipped a line along her neck.

Her knees jellied and she locked them, leaning into the wall for support.

She didn't need to. His hands grasped her hips, and he held her up.

And she was okay with that. Compromising wasn't losing herself in this case. Leaning on him, propping him up—they'd keep each other balanced.

"How about this?" she said. "I'll stay on the ropes rescue roster. But if it's preventing you from feeling well, you tell me. And I'll adjust."

"I thought I wouldn't be able to take chances again. I was wrong." He continued his torture along her collarbone.

"Okay, you may have had a point about going back to your place. We really should show our faces at the reception, I know, but we only need an hour…"

Another laugh erupted from his chest.

She dug her fingers into his shoulders and purposefully rubbed her hips against his hardening groin. "What?"

"An hour. On our first date, you asked me for an hour of my time."

She studied the humor dancing on his face, skepticism forcing her eyebrows up. "That's how you see that painful coffee meeting? A date?"

His shrug was unapologetic. "I'm in love. I'm allowed a little historical revisionism."

She'd allow him anything if he kept talking about being in love. Her smile softened to what had to be epic levels of smitten, but who cared? "Your point being?"

"You can have an hour."

She poked him in the chest. "I want more than that."

Seriousness erased the sparkle in his eyes, and his lips parted. "Far as I'm concerned, you can have forever."

After a long tangle of lips that left her short of breath, she leaned up to his ear. "Good. I don't plan on accepting anything less."

Epilogue

Caleb rushed up Evolve's front sidewalk with a larg polka-dot-papered box under one arm, cursing the tim glaring at him from his watch face. Damn it. Nothin; like arriving to a baby shower while the decorations wer being taken down to make a person feel like a heel. Bu the guest lecture he'd given to a class of medical student in Bozeman had dragged far longer than anticipated.

He couldn't entirely blame his lateness on work though. He'd had to make a stop on his way home, put ting him that much further behind. Good thing Garne had bought his excuse of traffic on that one. He wasn' sure if he was ready to share his purchase with her yet.

The little velvet box felt damn right in his pocket. An yeah, they'd talked about forever. But would she be o board with proving those words with a ring and som vows? He had yet to find the right moment to ask.

He slipped through the doors, trying to draw as littl attention as possible. A scattering of people still mille around the foyer. Garnet stood on the opposite side, talk ing with Lauren and Cadie by the unlit fireplace. A tiny pink bundle rested in Cadie's arms, and all three womer were gazing adoringly at the month-old infant. Enoug that when Garnet lifted her head, the vehemence of he glare and pointed look at the clock on the wall ove he pink-festooned reception desk was softened to half strength. Still, he wanted to give her a minute to simmer down before he interrupted and she spewed her wrath in his direction.

The reception desk wasn't the only thing decorated for the occasion. Pink littered the space, and he squinted at the onslaught, sidling over to Zach and Tavish, who were picking at the remains of a pastel-pink-iced cupcake tower on the food table.

"Sorry I'm late," he said, clapping his friends on the back and receiving a couple of whacks in return. He handed Tavish the gift. "Did a Pepto-Bismol factory explode in here?"

Tavish set the box on the table and shrugged, seeming to slough off both Caleb's lateness and the serious gender normativity going on with the decorations. "Cadie got carried away at the party store."

"She said she liked the break from the blue-and-white crap she's been buying for our wedding," Zach explained further, gazing longingly across the room at Cadie and her armful of baby.

That deserved some harassment. "Gonna pack away this pink bomb and hope to reuse it after you knock Cadie up?"

"I wish," Zach grumbled. "Been trying to convince her to get on that, but she's insistent she's going to be the first of her siblings *not* to have a baby on the way at the wedding. October cannot come soon enough. Count on seeing her at your practice by early next year."

"You're welcome to keep the streamers for yourself," Tavish offered with a grin. "Jazz up your office with those flower things."

Caleb shot his friend a dirty look, but his chest expanded a little as he did it. Nothing like getting close

enough to a group of guys so that they dished insul
your way.

Tavish's face blanked innocently. "Or maybe you ar
Garnet will have a girl."

Caleb waved off the suggestion. "We've only been s
rious for…" Trailing off, he followed his friend's pointe
look toward the women.

Oh. Holy crap. His already full chest expanded
bursting. He could get used to the sight of Garnet with
baby nestled in her arms and a radiant expression on he
face, lips pursed in that way parents did when they wer
cooing nonsense at an infant.

"We're not even engaged," he protested weakly.

Zach eyed him closely. "But you will be. Soon."

The ring in his pocket weighed a ton all of a sudder
"Damn right, we will."

Striding over to Garnet and her friends, he held h
hands up in an "I surrender" gesture. He winced at Lat
ren. "I'm so sorry I'm late."

She lifted a shoulder much like her husband had. "
haven't been on time for anything in four weeks."

"Yeah, but blow-outs and a wonky nap schedule a
far better reasons for tardiness than a few high achiev
ers with too many questions," he murmured, tracing
finger along Charlotte's impossibly soft cheek. The li
tle munchkin pursed her lips in her sleep, and Garnet l
out a soft sigh.

Yup, making a baby—more than one—with Ga
net was a damned necessity. He put his arm around he
shoulders and cuddled her into his side. "Not going t
lie, you're more attractive at this moment than you'v
ever been."

She shot him a dry look. "Even more than last wee
in the hot tub?"

He pretended to contemplate the two. "Tough choice. But yeah."

"You seriously got held up by students for two hours?" she whispered.

"Almost." He kissed her temple. "And I had an errand to run."

Her face darkened. "What errand could possibly matter more than our friends' baby shower? You didn't leave buying the gift until today, did you? You told me you had it taken—"

"The gift's been in my trunk for a week," he interrupted.

"So what was it then?"

"I'll explain later, okay?" He didn't want to steal the new parents' thunder, no matter how annoyed Garnet got.

"No, it's not okay." Her ability to simultaneously snap and whisper was truly impressive. "I get being held up at work. But what errand could have possibly been that important?"

"Oh, there are a few candidates."

"Babies outrank everything, except maybe a wedding..." She froze. "Caleb."

His heart raced. He usually loved her habit of saying whatever was on her mind, but in this particular moment, he needed her not to follow that instinct. "Garnet, not here."

"Are you *proposing*?"

The baby, who'd been quiet in Garnet's arms up until now, squawked. Out of the corner of his eye, he could see that Mackenzie Dawson and the middle-aged woman who ran the bakery were all of a sudden riveted to his and Garnet's conversation. As were Cadie and Lauren, who were now murmuring intently to each other.

"Wasn't planning on doing it here," he said, teeth gritted.

"You should!" Lauren exclaimed.

He raised his eyebrows at the new mom. "Seriously?"

She made a "get to it" motion with her hand.

Well, if one of the people of honor at this shindig felt it was appropriate, who was he to argue? Best to salvage the moment if he could. Reaching into his pocket, he pulled out the small jewelry box he'd picked up on his way here. He flicked the box open with his thumb before setting it on the baby's swaddled tummy. "This was my errand, Gigi."

The oval-cut garnet, set in a simple band, twinkled as it caught the light overhead.

Cadie and Lauren both oohed, and the conversation around the room ground to a halt.

But the only reaction he cared about was the one he *wasn't* getting from the woman he loved. She stood stock still, arms gripped around Charlotte and blank gaze fixed on the ring. Her mouth was a firm line. A pulse fluttered at her neck. She paled, making her freckles stand out more.

Crap. She wasn't ready. He'd screwed up, dropping this on her too early, and doubly so doing it in front of people she cared about.

"I know it's corny to buy you a stone you share a name with," he said in a rush. "And it's soon, I know, so if you want to wear it on your right hand, I get it…" Argh, he was bungling this. He took a deep breath. "I thought you might like something a little untraditional—"

"I do," she blurted, relaxing against his arm.

"That's what you're supposed to say at the ceremony, not during the proposal," he teased, the rush of relief over her agreement coming out as more of a joke than he'd intended.

She looked up at him, eyes sparkling with happy tears.

And you're supposed to actually ask me a question instead of assuming I'm going to say no."

He grinned. Plucking the ring out of the box, he held it near her left hand, the one tucked around the baby's tiny form.

"I'm going to want to make two or three of these little miracles, I think," he said.

"Okay, but that's not a question, either."

"Not particularly concerned about the marriage-baby order, so whatever works for—"

"A question, Caleb."

He bent to her ear. "I love you."

She growled.

"Be my wife?"

Her pause was enough to stop his heart.

"What if I want four kids?" she said.

"An answer, Garnet," he mimicked, chest shaking with laughter.

The corner of her mouth lifted. "I love you."

He held the ring at the tip of her finger.

"Yes." The word rang with promise and he slid the band past her knuckle. "Forever."

* * * * *

*Don't miss the previous titles in Laurel Greer's
Sutter Creek, Montana miniseries:*

From Exes to Expecting
A Father for Her Child

Available now from Harlequin Special Edition!

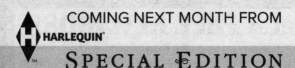

COMING NEXT MONTH FROM
HARLEQUIN'
SPECIAL EDITION

Available November 19, 2019

#2731 THE RIGHT REASON TO MARRY
The Bravos of Valentine Bay • by Christine Rimmer
Unexpected fatherhood changes everything for charming bachelor Liam Bravo.
wants to marry Karin Killigan, the mother of his child. But Karin won't settle for le
than true lasting love.

#2732 MAVERICK CHRISTMAS SURPRISE
Montana Mavericks: Six Brides for Six Brothers • by Brenda Harlen
Rancher Wilder Crawford is in no hurry to get married and start a family—until a
four-month-old baby is left on his doorstep on Christmas day!

#2733 THE RANCHER'S BEST GIFT
Men of the West • by Stella Bagwell
Rancher Matthew Waggoner was planning to be in and out of Red Bluff as
quickly as possible. But staying with his boss's sister, Camille Hollister, proves
to be more enticing than he thought. Will these two opposites be able to work
through their differences and get the best Christmas gift?

#2734 IT STARTED AT CHRISTMAS...
Gallant Lake Stories • by Jo McNally
Despite lying on her résumé, Amanda Lowery still manages to land a job design
Halcyon House for Blake Randall—and a place to stay over Christmas. Neither o
them have had much to celebrate, but with Blake's grieving nephew staying at
Halcyon, they're all hoping for some Christmas magic.

#2735 A TALE OF TWO CHRISTMAS LETTERS
Texas Legends: The McCabes • by Cathy Gillen Thacker
Rehab nurse Bess Monroe is mortified that she accidentally sent out two Christm
letters—one telling the world about her lonely life intead of the positive spin she
wanted! And when Jack McCabe, widowed surgeon and father of three, sees th
second one, he offers his friendship to get through the holidays. But their pact
soon turns into something more...

#2736 THE SOLDIER'S SECRET SON
The Culhanes of Cedar River • by Helen Lacey
When Jake Culhane comes home to Cedar River, he doesn't expect to reconn
with the woman he never forgot. Abby Perkins is still in love with the boy who
broke her heart when he enlisted. This could be their first Christmas as a real
family—if Abby can find the courage to tell Jake the truth.

HSECNM